BOY T

Sue Brown

CW01510424

Published by One Hat Press
Cover design by Pippa Wood
Formatting by Format4U/Clare London

A boy who's scared of being caged again. A Daddy who's about to rescue the world. Will they trust each other to fall in love when their future is unknown?

Throwing Jake and his brothers out of the Tin Bar seems like a good idea to Aaron. It avoids a fight with another Daddy, and he doesn't have to watch Jake play with another boy all evening.

Why does the guy who presses each one of Jake's Daddy buttons hate him so much? Jake's given up trying to attract his attention. Aaron clearly doesn't like him, and Jake needs to focus on the case.

Only Aaron's actions have unexpected consequences, and Jake brings his dream boy into the Brenner household. Aaron has good reason to avoid being caged. Can Jake persuade Aaron to wait for him or is it better to let his songbird go?

Contents

Chapter 1

Aaron

Aaron Yates was in hell. Absolute hell. He shouldn't even be working tonight, but one of the other bartenders was ill, and Pablo needed a cover urgently. It wasn't like Aaron couldn't do with the money. Working at the Tin Bar just about covered his rent and food, but he needed the extra shifts to survive.

Except for tonight. It was Tuesday night. Gay Daddies night at the Tin Bar. When all the Brenner boys from the Christmas tree farm on Kingdom Mountain descended on the bar, and took over the place with their bellowing voices and bushy beards. Who would believe seven huge bears of men would also turn out to be gay Daddies? The local boy population was in heaven.

Not Aaron though. He just considered the Brenners huge and annoying. He knew that was unfair and probably irrational. He didn't even mind most of them. Sure, Damien could be moody, although he was better now he'd gotten a boy of his own. The biggest one, PJ, was just an ass, although he had a ready smile for everyone, and the little twinks loved sitting on his lap or ass up, over it. No, it was Jake that was the problem.

Jake Brenner, the second to youngest brother, pushed every button Aaron had and then some. Aaron thought he was tall enough at a couple of inches under six foot. Although he was slender, he had muscles from working the bar. But Jake had at least ten inches on him and was three times the size. He had the same chestnut bushy hair and out-of-control beard most of the brothers had. He wore a blue plaid flannel shirt and jeans that had seen better days. The holes in the jeans could be distracting. Aaron dragged his gaze away from a hole too far up Jake's thigh, which showed exactly which way the bear dressed. He could see the same chestnut hair and a glimpse of bright red briefs peeking through the denim. Aaron was sure Jake had that fur all over. Aaron looked away. His penchant for furry men did not extend to Jake Brenner. At least that's what Aaron told himself.

Aaron did everything he could to avoid working Tuesday nights, even claiming that was the night he visited his granny, and he couldn't disappoint her. Pablo wasn't to know he didn't have a granny, to disappoint or otherwise. No, it was just that he wanted to avoid Jake Brenner and his revealing jeans.

It wasn't like Jake ever noticed he existed. Aaron was just the bartender, part of the furniture. Jake spent all his time with the sweet twinks, treating them so gently just as a Daddy should. This stupidly upset Aaron, especially when Jake gave him such a hard time if he got an order wrong. It was like Jake went out of his way to find something to yell at Aaron for. And then he'd go back to his twinks and treat them with gentle tenderness that made Aaron's gut twist in bitter knots.

So yeah, he avoided Tuesdays.

But Pablo had been desperate, and Aaron needed the money. His shift had never lasted so long. The brothers were drinking, which meant they weren't playing. They never drank alcohol when they were in a scene. But it didn't stop twinks draping themselves over the unattached brothers. Especially Jake. He seemed to attract them like flies on shit. Aaron was tempted to get out the fly swatter.

It didn't help the rest of the brothers had been pleased to see Aaron, especially Damien who'd thanked Aaron for his advice. Damien had been drowning his sorrows in the bar, and Aaron had told him to go home and sort it out with his boy before he caused a fight. It seemed like Damien had taken his advice because the big man didn't stop smiling all evening, even though his boy wasn't there with him. He had never seen Damien look so happy. Jake, on the other hand, wore a frown Aaron wasn't used to, and he sunk beer after beer until he was slurring his words and unsteady on his feet. It didn't stop a beautiful young man draping himself over Jake's lap and Jake didn't push him off. Aaron gritted his teeth and tried to focus on the customers and not the Daddy of his dreams.

The brothers got louder as they got drunker. Elements of the conversation drifted over to where Aaron was tending bar. They seemed to be talking about a road trip. They were excited and worried about the trip at the same time. Aaron made sure they didn't see the look on his face. He knew most of the brothers had rarely been off the mountain. They had been born in the huge cabin halfway up Kingdom mountain, and still lived there together.

They didn't know how lucky they were. The brothers had a home and a family. Aaron had neither. He had spent the last seven years on the road, moving from job to job, never staying anywhere long enough to put down roots. This town was the longest he'd ever stayed in one place. Maybe it was time he moved on. It wasn't fair on Jake that he had the problem. Or maybe it would be easier when they left. Jake was one of the brothers going on the road trip, and Aaron would be able to breathe again when he didn't have to watch Jake love on every boy except him.

Aaron was in the middle of serving a tiny, nervous twink when there was a sudden screech, and then a roar. He looked over to see the brothers on their feet. Oh hell, what had happened in the minute he'd not been gazing at Jake?

A table was upturned, and pints of beer spilled onto the carpet. Great, that was gonna be fun to clear up. Jake was facing off with another guy Aaron knew was also a daddy. Jake was twice the size of the other Daddy, but the guy was riled up. Jake looked wonderful, with flashing blue eyes, and bulging muscles from his clenched fists. But he wouldn't hit the other man unless the guy went for him. Then all bets were off. Aaron had been here before. He didn't miss the excited expression in the boy's eyes. Jake had put the boy behind him, to protect him as a Daddy should. What he didn't realize was that this man was the boy's Daddy. The boy had been playing him. He wanted to start a fight.

Dammit. Aaron had to cut this off before someone—Jake—spent the night behind bars or in the ER. He stormed around the bar and headed to the warring duo, holding his hand up as one of the brothers started to explain.

"I don't care who started it. You pick up the glasses and the bottles and take them over to the bar. You're all cut off for the night. I'm not barring you, but you need to get out of here."

"You can't do that," Jake spluttered, scowling at Aaron.

Aaron glowered at him. "I damn well can." He pointed at the boy. "This kid is playing you, Jake. He belongs to the other Daddy." Then Aaron turned on the guy who had started the fight. "Keep your boy and your fists under control. If he does it again both of you are barred." Aaron looked at the kid, who still looked disappointed that there hadn't been a fight. "This isn't how you treat a Daddy. You should have more respect for him than that."

He caught Jake's speculative expression. Now what? But Jake didn't say anything.

Aaron waited for them to pick up the table and the glasses, and then shuffle out of the bar. Jake seemed…well, kind of angry but also hurt, but one of the other brothers clapped a hand on his shoulder and hustled him out of the bar before he could protest any further. Damien stopped and turned back to Aaron.

"I'm sorry about Jake. He's not normally an asshole like this, but he's had really bad news about the case we're working on. I think it's upset him."

For a second Aaron felt guilty and thought about calling them back, but it was too late. All the brothers were gone, and Aaron was left with a quiet bar and the mess to clean up.

Aaron groaned as his phone rang in his ear. He fumbled for the phone and managed to connect it before voicemail kicked in.

"Yeah?" he slurred.

"What the hell were you doing, boy?"

He got stuck on the 'boy' and it took Aaron a moment to realize it was his boss yelling at him. "Pablo? What's wrong? What did I do?"

"You threw the Brenners out of the bar."

"They were about to have a fight," Aaron said. "Jake was playing with another man's boy."

"I don't care what they were doing or who he was playing with," Pablo snapped. "You don't throw the Brenners out. Dammit, Aaron, you should know this."

Aaron was slow to catch up. He squinted at the clock and realized he'd only had four hours sleep. "Pablo…" he started.

"This is the second time you've thrown out one

of the brothers," his boss roared. "These guys drink, Aaron. They pay the bills. You can't just throw them out like they're any random customer. I'm sorry, son, but that was your last shift at the Tin Bar."

Aaron sat up, Pablo's words penetrating his sleep-hazed brain. "You're firing me? For doing my job?"

"You've had it in for the Brenners ever since you arrived. I don't know what your problem is, but I can't deal with it. I'm sorry, Aaron, but we're done. Come get your pay this morning." Pablo disconnected the call.

Aaron sat up in bed and stared at the phone. He'd stopped a fight and lost his job? What the fuck? He'd lost his job because of fucking Jake Brenner. What the hell was he going to do now? He couldn't afford this room unless he worked. Yeah, the room was a shithole, but it was his. He didn't have a nice cozy cabin up in the mountains. Aaron's lip curled as he thought about who did.

Dammit, he guessed the decision about his future was made for him. Maybe it was for the best. Being near Jake Brenner was making him sour. Aaron wasn't usually like that about any man. He was an easy-going guy, ready with a smile for anyone. Now he wasn't smiling. He had two options. He could find another job in town, or he could take this as a sign and move on.

Aaron nodded to himself. It was time to go.

Two hours later he had his last pay in his pocket, an apology from Pablo but not his job back, and he was ready to leave. He'd hitchhike out of town and take the first vehicle that stopped for him. He didn't have any responsibilities and he could go where the wind took him as long as it wasn't back to *her*.

He stuck out his thumb as a truck came toward him.

Success!

The vehicle pulled up ahead of him. He jogged to the truck and opened the door.

A middle-aged, balding guy smiled at him. "Where do you want to go, son?"

"Wherever you're going as long as it's a long way from here," Jake said as he climbed in.

The trucker chuckled. "Did you get a girl pregnant? Are you running away?"

Aaron rolled his eyes. "I'm running away, but from a guy, not a girl."

He wasn't sure exactly what happened next. He heard the yell, but he didn't see the punch coming. His head cracked back, and seeing stars, he wasn't prepared for the driver to shove him out of the truck and onto the road. He hit the ice packed ground hard, the breath forced out of him from the impact.

Aaron watched the lights tear down the road and fade away. He was left dazed at the side of the road, blood dripping onto the ice, the crimson pattern almost hypnotic. It was too dangerous to remain here. He needed to find another ride. But Aaron's head ached more with every breath, and he felt sick. He'd stay where he was until he worked up the energy to move.

Jake

Jake groaned as he relaxed in the tub. After the brouhaha at the bar, which wasn't his fault really, he'd almost lost bath privileges. He'd had to do some fast talking with Vinny to keep them. Damien and Vinny let the brothers use the big tub when they wanted to. Most of the time Jake used a shower in his own bathroom, but there was nothing like stretching out in the tub with bubbles and boy fantasies. It would be his last bath before they went on the road for months, and he was going to make the most of it.

Despite his desire to do nothing more than dream about sharing the tub with a fantasy boy, his mind kept returning to the previous night. Jake was still incredulous about being thrown out of the Tin Bar. It was hardly his fault the young boy had draped all over him. He thought it was a pleasant interlude, nothing more. His brothers had laid into him on the way home for wrecking their night out. Jake protested it wasn't his fault. How was he to know the boy was already claimed? Jake knew he deserved a shiner from the boy's Daddy. He would have done the same thing if it had been his boy.

But the kicker was Damien who took him aside when they reached the cabin and pointed out that he was hurting Aaron. Jake had just stared at him, and Damien had sighed.

"You really are oblivious, Jake. Open your eyes."

That was rich, considering how blind Damien

had been to Vinny's affections, but Damien had just patted his shoulder and told him to apologize to Aaron. Then he'd left him standing in the snow.

Jake bit his lip. The bartender had been on his case from the moment they met. The guy was all smiles and laughter for his brothers, but one look at Jake and Aaron just glowered at him. What was the guy's problem? Jake tried to stay away from him. He didn't see him most Tuesdays. Now he wondered if that was Aaron's choice. Was Aaron avoiding him?

The boy was beautiful. Lean with thick, wavy hair and huge, dark blue eyes. But Jake wasn't willing to pursue anyone who wasn't eager. Jake was usually very careful about who he chose to be his boys and he rarely brought them home. His brothers weren't so particular, but Jake kept his dalliances away from the kitchen.

Just the thought of Aaron made Jake's cock stiffen. He and Aaron weren't meant to be, but maybe he could have his fantasy in the tub though. He wrapped his hand around his cock and squeezed gently.

"Jake, sorry, I need—shit, did you have to be doing that when I looked in?" Alec barked at him.

Jake gaped at his older brother and partner-in-crime in their private investigation business. "This is my time alone. Get lost. And a dollar."

He wasn't embarrassed to be caught with his hand around his cock. With seven brothers, it wasn't the first time. But this was his tub time, not Alec's.

Alec grimaced and dug in his pockets, bringing

out a dollar. "Sorry, but PJ needs a hand to get a final consignment of logs to town."

"Now?" Jake grumbled. "This is my time. What about Damien or Brad. Or even Harry if you can drag him away from the stables."

Alec rolled his eyes. "Quit whining and get your butt out of the tub instead of fantasizing about your boy. Whichever boy you're thinking about. We need to do something useful for once." He stood there and tapped his foot.

Jake wasn't going to get his bubble time for masturbatory fun. He growled as he climbed out of the tub. If he had to do this, he was gonna claim another bath before they left. He shoved Alec toward the door and grabbed a towel. So much for a lazy morning.

It didn't take long to transport the logs. His brother had just needed extra muscle. PJ thanked Jake and Alec and then went to hunt down chow for lunch. Alec had a lead he wanted to pursue, and Jake decided to get lunch at the bar he'd been at the previous night. The brothers went their separate ways. Jake had come in his old Ford pickup so he could do his own thing. Damien's conversation from the previous night weighed on his mind. If Aaron was doing the early shift at the Tin Bar, Jake would go apologize to him. He owed Aaron that.

The bar was almost empty when he went inside, just a few guys doing their crosswords with a half-empty glass of beer in front of them. There was no sign of Aaron, but Jake went up and smiled at Pablo.

"Hey, Pablo, is Aaron around? I want to say sorry for last night."

Pablo shook his head. "I fired his sorry ass for being rude to you." He didn't look happy about it though as he wiped down the bar.

Jake frowned, taken aback. "Why did you fire him? I thought you liked him."

"I do. I did. But I can't have bar staff being rude to paying customers. You guys are good customers. I don't want to drive you away." He looked expectantly at Jake as if he should be pleased with Pablo's decision.

But Jake felt gutted and upset for Aaron's sake. He knew the guy had issues with him, but Aaron didn't deserve to be fired for it, and he had prevented a fight. If anyone should be barred from the bar, it should be the kid who started the whole thing. He was definitely gonna have a word with the boy's Daddy about that.

Jake wanted to leave, but Pablo had put a beer in front of him. So he had the one drink and left as quickly as he could. The last thing he wanted to do was negotiate the mountain road intoxicated.

As he drove to the outskirts of the town, Aaron's fate rested uneasily in his mind. Jake wondered whether Aaron would find another job in the town. There were a couple of other bars although the Tin Bar was the only gay establishment. Come to that, he didn't even know if Aaron was gay. But there was nothing he could do about it now. He had to focus his attention on the Kingdom Mountain theme park mess. They were almost ready to go on the road trip and Jake had a lot of work to do before then.

He was about to turn off to the mountain road leading to the cabin when he spotted a heap of clothes at the side of the highway. Jake huffed, hating that people just dumped their trash. He hopped out of the pickup, deciding he'd take the clothes home and see if they could be reused. Brad liked blowing things up.

But when he bent over the pile, he discovered it wasn't a heap of old clothes. It was a young guy. For a moment, Jake had the sick feeling he used to get when they found a young man frozen to death in their woods. Before Lyle joined their family. Before they understood what 'disappeared' truly meant to the boys of Kingdom Mountain.

The guy moaned, and the sick feeling intensified, as Jake realized it was Aaron.

As Jake knelt beside him, Aaron groaned again. "My God. What happened to you, boy? Where did you get that bruise on your face?"

He didn't think too much of the way 'boy' slipped out. He was more concerned about Aaron.

Aaron opened his eyes, blinking as if he couldn't focus on Jake. "Jake? Where am I? Do you want a beer?"

"You're on the road out of town, not in the bar. What happened to you?"

Aaron licked his lips. He tried to sit up. Jake put an arm around him and encouraged Aaron to lean against Jake's chest. Aaron didn't seem to have the energy to protest.

"Truck," Aaron muttered.

At least that's what Jake thought he said. He wasn't entirely sure. "How long have you been here?"

"Since he hit me." Aaron didn't sound too sure.

"Who hit you?" Jake was ready to go up in flames at the thought of anyone hurting his boy. He took a deep breath. Not *his* boy. Just a boy in need.

"Truck."

Jake shook his head. He couldn't leave Aaron here. He could die of hypothermia or get run over. "You're coming with me."

Aaron struggled, trying to push him away. "Can't. Nowhere to go."

"You can come back to the cabin. I can't leave you here, Aaron. You'll die if I leave you."

"It doesn't matter. No one would care."

The boy was going to wrench his heart. Jake pressed a kiss on the top of Aaron's head. "I'd care. Come on."

Jake manhandled Aaron to his feet and got him into the pickup with some difficulty. He slung Aaron's pack into the back and went around to the driver's side. Aaron leaned against the passenger door, his eyes closed. Jake wasn't sure whether he was sleeping or unconscious, but he didn't move as Jake started the vehicle. Jake wondered whether he should take Aaron to the ER, but the cabin was closer, and Harry was cheaper. They were still paying off the medical bills from Gruff's visit when he was poisoned.

Aaron didn't move or open his eyes, so Jake drove as carefully as he could up the mountain road.

He slammed the pickup into park outside the cabin, and hurried around to the passenger door, carefully opening it so Aaron didn't fall onto the ice.

Aaron opened his eyes, saw Jake, and tried to push him away again. "Leave me alone."

"Calm down, boy," Jake snapped. The last thing he wanted to do was drop Aaron. His brothers would never let him forget it. To his surprise Aaron subsided and allowed Jake to ease him out of the pickup. Aaron took one step and wobbled.

Jake rolled his eyes and swept Aaron up into his arms before the boy broke something. He hurried up the stoop and into the cabin, appreciating the blast of hot air. Damien and Gruff sat at the kitchen table. As Jake came in with his burden, they exchanged a look.

"And another one," Damien muttered, and Gruff nodded.

Jake frowned. "What do you mean by that?"

"I'll tell you later," Damien said. "You need to take care of your boy."

"He's not my—"

Gruff patted his shoulder. "Take him upstairs."

They didn't even question why he was here. But then, Aaron wasn't the first unconscious boy to arrive at the cabin.

Jake hurried up the stairs, but hesitated at the top, unsure where to put him. He was about to go into the little room which had been Vinny's, when Vinny and Lyle approached him.

"Put him in your bedroom," Vinny said. "He

needs you."

Jake wasn't sure exactly what he meant by that, but Lyle nodded as if he agreed. Jake took him into his bedroom and laid him on his unmade bed. Then he realized how wet Aaron's clothes were. He couldn't leave his boy like that. He undressed Aaron carefully, throwing all his wet clothes into the bathroom. He was sure he could find something for Aaron to wear later. Then he tucked Aaron up in the comforter.

He looked up at a knock at the door and Harry poked his head around.

"I hear I've got another patient."

Jake stood back so that Harry could examine Aaron, although he was strangely reluctant to allow Harry to touch him. "It looks like he's taken a beating."

"Did he say what happened?"

Jake shook his head. "Something to do with a trucker. He kind of passed out after that."

"I think he'll be fine once he warms up," Harry examined Aaron carefully, although Jake breathed a sigh of relief when Harry had finished. "He's probably gonna have a headache when he wakes up."

"This is getting to be a habit, finding boys in the snow," Jake said. "Did you know Pablo fired him?"

Harry turned to look at him. "You serious? Why? Aaron was his best bartender."

"Because he was rude to us and threw us out."

Harry's eyebrows raised almost comically. "So Aaron was leaving town because he had nowhere to go?"

"It seems like it."

"Another homeless boy. We really are making a habit of it. I wonder where I'll find mine."

"In a stable probably," Jake said, pointing out Harry's love of horses. "Now go away and let me take care of my...Aaron."

Harry snorted, but he did leave them alone. Jake looked down at the bartender in his bed. "What on earth am I going to do with you, sweet boy?"

Chapter 2

Aaron

Aaron awoke, confused about where he was. He hadn't opened his eyes but even without sight, he knew the bed didn't feel like his own. It was comfortable and squishy, and the bed clothes pressed down on him making him feel over-warm. He'd gotten used to being cold in his room. Even the smell of the laundry detergent was wrong. He used a lemon-scented detergent, and this was lavender.

All these thoughts ran through his head, but the main one was why did his face hurt so much? He pressed where the pain was centered.

"Ouch!"

"Don't do that."

Jake?

Aaron's eyes snapped open to find the big bear leaning over him, his expression concerned.

"How do you feel?" Jake asked.

He looked amazing, and Aaron wanted nothing more than to wrap his arms around Jake's neck. Then reality reasserted itself.

"What the hell am I doing here?" Aaron yelled. Then he looked down at himself. "And why am I naked? Did you kidnap me and bring me home? God, haven't you people ever heard of consent?"

Jake's eyes grew wider and wider during his tirade and then they narrowed. "Enough," he snapped. "I appreciate you may be feeling confused, but you don't get to accuse me of kidnap, when all I did was save your goddamn life."

"You did?" Aaron frowned and then wished he hadn't because that really hurt. "You had me fired."

Jake had the grace to look embarrassed. "I had no idea Pablo was going to fire you. I told him that this morning."

"You spoke to Pablo?" Aaron was getting more and more confused. "You never go to the bar in the morning."

Jake took a deep breath, feeling this conversation was about to spiral out of his control. "I went to the bar to apologize to you for last night. I was out of order. It's been a rough couple of weeks. If I'd had my head on straight, I would have known that the kid was just playing me."

"Damien said things had been bad." Wait, why was he sticking up for Jake? Aaron hated Jake.

Jake nodded. "It has, but I'm sorry you got caught in the middle of it. I can talk to Pablo and try to make him change his mind."

"There's no point. I'll always be waiting for the next time he tries to fire me. I've been here too long. It's about time I moved out and found somewhere new."

Aaron would never trust Pablo again. No, it was

better to find a new place to work. Besides, it was damn cold here in the winter. He knew that from the last time. He could find somewhere which didn't freeze his balls off.

Jake didn't look convinced, but he nodded. "Well, you're not going anywhere at the moment until Harry gives you the all-clear."

Aaron wrinkled his forehead and again wished he hadn't. "Isn't Harry your brother who likes horses?"

"He's the nearest thing we've got to a doctor." Jake grinned. "He isn't anything like a doctor, but he's all we've got."

Aaron needed to get out of here. He sat up and his head spun. He moaned and then he had a solid chest to lean against and arms like tree trunks around him, holding him in place. He had the urge to beg Jake to never let him go.

"Just relax, Aaron," Jake murmured. "You don't have to rush anywhere. Why don't you go back to sleep, and I'll bring you food when you wake up next time? Lyle makes really good soup."

Even the thought of soup made Aaron's stomach roil, but he knew Jake was trying to make him feel better. He lay down on the pillows and looked around the room. He would have known this was Jake's bedroom from the huge plaid shirts flung over every surface. Aaron had seen Jake wearing most of them.

Jake bent over him and brushed Aaron's hair back from his face in an oddly tender gesture. "I know everything seems strange at the moment, but you'll feel better soon."

"It's not the first time I've been hit," Aaron muttered.

Jake's expression darkened. He didn't seem to like that answer at all. But he didn't say anything and just left the bedroom. Aaron lay there for a long moment. He knew he should get up, get dressed, and get out of there. But for some reason his head was telling him to shut up and go to sleep. It seemed like a really good idea so for once Aaron listened to his head and closed his eyes.

When he woke up for the second time, it was dark in the bedroom. Aaron sat up and sucked in a deep breath as a wave of nausea rolled over him. Dammit, he should be feeling better now.

"Still feeling dizzy, huh?" Jake said.

Aaron blinked as Jake switched on a lamp on the nightstand. He hadn't realized Jake was in the room. "You were sitting in the dark?"

"Playing on my phone." Jake held it up to show Aaron. "I didn't want to disturb you. How are you feeling?"

Aaron decided to avoid that question. "What time is it?" he asked.

Jake's eyes narrowed. He obviously noted the deflection. "It's eight o'clock."

"In the evening?" Aaron was aghast. He'd slept all day.

"In the evening," Jake confirmed, sounding amused.

"I've got to—"

"You haven't got to do anything." Jake pushed Aaron back onto the pillows. "You're not going anywhere tonight. If you try to get down the mountain road, you'll probably fall off the edge."

"I can't sleep here," Aaron protested, although he was very comfortable and if it had been anyone else's bed, he'd have been pleased at the invitation to stay.

Jake raised an eyebrow. "Why not?"

"This is your bed."

Now Jake looked amused again. "It's a very big bed. I'm sure we could share it. Or there's a small bed next door I can sleep in. It's small but I suppose I could manage," he added almost plaintively.

Aaron couldn't help looking to the side. Jake was right. It really was a big bed. But even so Aaron wasn't exactly enthused by the idea of sharing with the man of his dreams. With his luck he'd spend all night with a boner or wake up with his dick pushed against Jake's asscrack.

"Why don't you come down with me to the kitchen and get food?" Jake said.

Aaron pushed back the bed close and got to his feet. He swayed but Jake was right there by his side, ready to catch him if necessary. "I need a leak," he muttered.

"Okay," Jake said cheerfully.

Jake walked him to the bathroom door but, to Aaron's relief, didn't seem to want to join him in the bathroom. Aaron pushed the door closed and took a long look at himself in the mirror. He was a mess. He had a black eye, now swollen shut, and the bruising spread down his cheek and across his nose. However he'd gotten the black eye, the man must have punched him with deadly accuracy. He suddenly had a memory of sitting in the truck, then his head snapping back and ending up on the road. It didn't take much to piece it together. He'd gone hitchhiking and it hadn't ended up with him in a new town.

"Are you okay in there?" Jake called.

"I'm fine," Aaron called back.

He used the john and then washed his hands. He desperately wanted a shower, but he didn't think he had enough energy to do that, so he splashed water on his face and patted it dry.

When Aaron returned to the bedroom, Jake had remade the bed and was waiting for him by the door. "Just a warning my brothers are down there. You know them all, of course."

Serving them in the bar and meeting them in their home, were two different things.

"I need something to wear," he said. He wasn't going to walk downstairs naked.

Jake picked up a pile of clothes on the dresser. "These are yours. Clean and dry."

"You laundered my clothes?"

"Mine would be too big and the boys are smaller than you. I didn't have time to hunt through the chests in the attic."

Aaron had no idea what Jake was talking about, but he couldn't stay in Jake's bedroom forever, so he dressed and let Jake lead him down the stairs. Jake was ahead of him so didn't see Aaron's stunned expression at the size of the cabin. With seven brothers and two boys living here, they could hardly live in a tiny one-story. He wondered how they managed to live together without wanting to kill each other. He'd only shared with one other person, and he'd wanted to kill them every single day of his life.

In the kitchen, eight pairs of eyes snapped to look at him as they walked in.

"Don't be assholes," Jake said to everyone, and led Aaron to an empty chair. "Rexy, leave him alone."

Rexy was a young black dog with a white patch on his chest, who rushed over to greet them. Aaron gingerly bent down to pet the dog, trying not to grimace at the pain that shot through his head.

"Rexy, over here."

The order came from one of the three men that Aaron didn't recognize. They were nearer his age. To his surprise, the dog obeyed. Aaron was sure one of the older brothers was missing too.

A young man, much like the twinks at the bar, smiled at him. "Would you like a bowl of soup?"

Aaron still wasn't sure how settled his stomach was, but he managed a smile because he didn't want to offend the sweet boy. "Thanks." He looked around the table again. "One of you isn't here. Is it Brad?"

"That's right," Jake said. "He's probably in one of the barns. He likes blowing things up."

"And then writing poetry about it," Gruff said.

Aaron stared at them, wondering if this was a joke at his expense.

"He really does do that," Jake assured him. "We've got our own hobbies. Brad is just weirder than most."

Aaron stared down at the bowl of rich vegetable soup that was placed in front of him. He wasn't sure he could eat it. His mouth hurt so much.

"Just try," Jake said, nudging him a little. You don't have to eat it all."

Aaron dipped his spoon in the bowl and inhaled the rich aroma of the soup. His stomach rumbled a little. Maybe he could try a spoon or two. The taste was amazing, and he said so, getting a broad smile from the boy who had served him the soup.

"I'm trying new recipes," the boy said.

"This is Lyle," Jake said. "He belongs to Gruff. Vinny here belongs to Damien. And this is Matt who was sensible enough to stay clear of all of us, but he's part of the big case we're on."

Aaron hadn't spent six years tending bar to be stupid. He could read faces and knew most of what Jake said about Matt was wrong. Matt wasn't there for the big case. He was there for Alec, and Alec alone. It didn't take him long to realize that Alec felt exactly the same way about Matt. They just had no way to communicate that to each other. Aaron carried on eating the soup. It was none of his business who liked who or what. He would be out of there by the next morning, far away from the Brenners.

Jake

Jake knew his brothers weren't happy about the

timing of Aaron's arrival. But he couldn't have left his boy lying in the snow. He would have been dead by morning. Jake's brain caught up to the 'his boy' too late.

The silence around the table was painful and they all stared at each other. This was getting ridiculous. They were never this quiet. Jake caught Damien's eye. His older brother shrugged.

Aaron looked up from the soup bowl. "Do you want me to go away? One of you could give me a ride into town."

Jake stared at him. "What?"

"You're not talking. You guys never shut up. I'm fine now. I'll leave you to talk." Aaron put down his spoon and stood. "Thanks for the soup, Lyle."

Hell no!

Jake sprang to his feet and pushed Aaron down. "It's dark. You're not going anywhere now, boy."

He only realized what he'd said when Aaron's eyes went wide.

Oh crap.

How was Jake going to dig himself out of this hole? He didn't risk a glance at his brothers. The silence was enough.

Jake sighed and sat next to Aaron. "I'm sorry, Aaron. Don't go anywhere tonight."

"You need to talk," Aaron sounded a little breathless.

"We can talk any time," Jake assured him.

"Jake—" Damien started.

"Is it about your Kingdom theme parks road trip?" Aaron asked.

Nine jaws dropped open.

"What the hell?" Alec snapped. "How the hell do you know about that?"

Aaron rolled his eyes. "Me, bartender. You, guys with big mouths."

Jake was sure he heard an indelicate snort, and a hissed "Boy!" from Damien.

"He's right though," Vinny muttered sullenly.

Alec glowered at Aaron. "You overheard us?"

"I'm a bartender. Most people treat me as if I'm deaf."

The way Aaron avoided looking at Jake told Jake he had been one of those people.

"So what do you know?" Jake asked.

"You're on a mission to save all the orphan boys." Aaron was smiling but it didn't reach his eyes.

"You got a problem with that, bartender?" Vinny snapped.

Aaron turned to look at Damien's boy who was scowling at him. "It makes no difference to me. Every boy needs a savior."

Why did that sound so bitter? Had Aaron needed a savior when he was a boy? It didn't sound as if he meant today.

Before Jake could press him, Aaron said, "If it's okay, I want to go to bed, Jake. My head is hurting. It's been a long day."

Jake went to stand, but Aaron pushed him down. "You stay and talk. I know the way. Thanks for the soup."

He left the room and Jake stared after him. When he turned back all the men around the table were staring at him.

"What?"

"Go after him, idiot," PJ hissed.

"Why? We have to talk."

"You called him your boy," Alec pointed out.

"It was a slip of the tongue."

"Not to him it wasn't. Go sort it out," Damien said, and his boy nodded.

Jake scowled at his brothers. "We've got to discuss the road trip."

"We can do that. You can catch up when your boy's asleep," Alec said. "And he needs Tylenol. His face is pinched and under the bruising, he's whiter than snow."

Jake huffed but he got to his feet. He wasn't going to get away with not talking to Aaron. Dammit. Why hadn't he been more cautious? He was just so used to saying boy. He forgot other men got offended by it.

When he entered his bedroom, the light was out, but he could see by the light from the hall that Aaron was already in bed, his back and shoulders above the comforter. Jake's mouth went dry at the bare skin and curve of muscles.

"Aaron?" he murmured.

"I'm fine," Aaron muttered, but he didn't turn to face Jake. "Go back to your brothers."

"I don't take orders from boys," Jake growled, then smacked his head. He was supposed to be apologizing, not repeating the error.

"I'm not your boy," Aaron pointed out.

An apology hovered on Jake's tongue. Then he saw how still Aaron was, as if he were barely breathing.

Is that what Aaron wanted? To be a boy? Or did he want to be Jake's boy?

Jake sat down on the bed, close but not touching. He wasn't going to be yelled at for non-consent again. He looked at the rigid line of Aaron's back. "But you'd like to be, wouldn't you?"

"I don't know what you're talking about."

This time Jake grinned at the indifference in Aaron's voice. The boy was lying through his teeth. "Do you want a Daddy, Aaron? Is that it? All the time you've been at the bar watching the Daddies and boys, and you wanted a Daddy of your own."

The silence stretched out for a long time.

"So what if I did?" Aaron whispered, and his need made Jake's heart ache.

"Have you ever had a Daddy, boy?"

"Not really." The words sounded as if they were torn out of Aaron's soul.

Jake wished he could see Aaron's expression. "Why not?"

"Because I never stayed anywhere long enough."

Jake frowned. "But you've been at the Tin Bar for ages."

"I liked it there. Mostly."

"Except for the Daddy/boy nights," Jake hazarded.

Aaron sighed and rolled over onto his back. "It was hard. Seeing the Daddies pick up the boys and never look at me."

"Maybe they didn't know you were a boy," Jake

suggested gently. "I had no idea."

Aaron stared up at the ceiling. "I know you didn't." He sounded so defeated.

Jake reached out to touch him, then pulled his hand back. "Aaron."

But Aaron didn't look at him.

"I expect my boys to look at me when I talk to them." Jake let the edge to his tone seep through.

"At the risk of repeating myself, I'm not your boy. I know the type you like. All sweet and twinky."

"You know nothing about what I like," Jake said.

Aaron barked out a laugh. "I spent a year watching you every week, remember. I know exactly what kind of boys you like."

Was that a touch of jealousy in Aaron's voice? He still refused to look at Jake.

"You saw the boys draped themselves over me. Did you ever see me choose a boy?"

Aaron furrowed his brow. "Uh...no."

"Because those boys were just looking for a good time for the evening. It was fun, nothing more." Jake leaned forward. "If you had looked carefully, you'd have realized I was too busy looking in the direction of a man I didn't know was a boy. One who didn't even notice I existed."

Aaron rolled over to face him, his hands under his cheek. "He noticed. He just thought you weren't looking."

They stared at each other for a long moment.

Jake observed how pinched Aaron looked. Matt had been right. "On a scale of one to ten, how much pain are you in?"

Aaron gave a wry smile. "Twenty."

Jake cursed himself. He should have given Aaron the Tylenol instead of the third degree. He got off the bed and headed into the bathroom. He returned with the pain meds and a glass of water, and put both on the nightstand.

He looked at Aaron. "I'm going to help you sit up. Don't yell at me."

Aaron had the grace to blush. "I won't."

Jake put an arm around Aaron's back and eased him into a sitting position. He heard Aaron's gasp. "What's wrong?"

"Feeling sick," Aaron bit out through gritted teeth.

Jake dumped the contents of the trash can on the floor and handed it to Aaron. Then he sat carefully on the bed behind the boy. "Lean against me for a moment. See if it eases."

Aaron took a deep breath before he leaned against Jake. They sat like that for a long while and Jake wondered if Aaron had dozed off until he suddenly spoke.

"I don't think I'm gonna hurl," Aaron murmured.

"Let's see how you are after taking the Tylenol." Jake handed him the tablets and water which Aaron took, then he eased Aaron back against him. "You can lie down in a moment."

"I don't think I ever want to move," Aaron murmured.

Jake kissed the top of Aaron's head. "You don't have to, my boy. You can sleep like this all night if you want to."

Chapter 3

Aaron

Aaron closed his eyes and leaned against Jake's chest, hearing the *thump thump* of Jake's heart under his ear. His head pounded but the nausea had eased. He wasn't in a rush to move though, just in case.

He was still bemused by the day. He woke up to be fired from his job because of Jake Brenner, he was thumped by a homophobe, and he ended the day in Jake Brenner's bed, being held in his arms as if he were something precious and being called his boy. He wasn't sure how it happened, but he was going to make the most of the one night he had like this. Tomorrow Aaron would be on the road again. Tonight he could pretend that he was loved and this was his home.

Jake's arms were warm and solid, and he didn't seem in any rush to let Aaron go. His plaid shirt was soft under his cheek. Aaron wished it was his bare chest. He'd seen Jake shirtless once when a drunk boy tried to strip him. Jake had only let him go so far, but Aaron had seen the thick chestnut curls on Jake's chest, and he'd wanted to wrench the boy off and be the one to rub all over Jake like a cat.

Still, it was right that he was the one naked and Jake was dressed. He was the boy, and Jake was the Daddy. Jake didn't seem to mind Aaron being in his arms like this.

He didn't know how long they'd sat there when he heard a knock at the door. Aaron buried his face in Jake's shirt. He didn't want Jake to leave, but he guessed he was being called back to the meeting.

"Just seeing how my patient is."

That was Harry. Aaron knew his rumble. He knew all their voices although he'd never tell them that.

"He was feeling sick, and his head is bad."

Aaron heard the concern in Jake's voice and felt bad he'd made him worry. He raised his head to look at Harry and felt a wave of dizziness rush over him. He swallowed hard and tried again. "I'm okay." It didn't sound convincing, even to him, and he rested his head against Jake again.

"Jake, may I examine your boy?" Harry asked.

That was...oddly formal. And aimed at Jake, not him.

"Aaron?" Jake's voice was soft. "Harry's just going to check you over. Okay?"

He whimpered at the thought of moving from Jake's arms, but Harry said, "You stay where you are, Aaron. Jake can hold you."

Harry's hands were gentle on him and didn't last long. "The guy had a solid right hook, hmm?"

"I didn't even see it coming," Aaron admitted. It was embarrassing but he'd been so intent on getting on the road, he'd never looked at the trucker.

"I'm just going to shine a bright light in your eyes," Harry said.

The light made Aaron want to hurl and Jake growled, but Harry told him to calm down. "Your pupils are fine. I think a night's sleep and you'll feel much better, but Jake can call me if you get any worse."

Aaron was relieved Harry didn't want to send him to the ER. Jake's arms tightened around him reassuringly and he crooned something in Aaron's ear. Aaron was sure Jake said he'd never let him go, but he couldn't be sure.

"You can go away now," Jake said pointedly.

Harry snorted and left them alone. Aaron tried to move but Jake didn't let him go.

"Do you need a leak?" Jake asked.

"No."

"Are you gonna vomit?"

"Uh...no." If Aaron didn't think about that too much, he was fine.

"Then we'll stay like this until you're ready to sleep."

"But—"

"Boy, close your eyes and rest."

It was an order and Aaron gave up the fight. He closed his eyes and let himself be lulled by the sound of Jake's heart.

Aaron woke to a heated discussion conducted in low voices. When he opened his eyes, it took him a moment to realize where he was, but then he remembered he was in the cabin. The bed was empty apart from him, so one of those voices was probably Jake.

"We've got to get on the road. We can't hang about here, just because you want to play nursemaid." That was Alec and he sounded pissed off.

"We weren't going to leave for a few days," Jake pointed out. "Aaron should be feeling better by then."

"But Ryder's information changes things. We've got to move the dates up, Jake. The RVs are ready. We should go today."

"But Aaron might not be well enough," Jake hissed.

"Then Harry can take care of him."

No! Aaron tried to sit up, but he had to wait as his head and stomach both protested. He looked around and found the trash can at the side of the bed. He grabbed it just in case.

"Isn't gonna happen," Jake said flatly. "If we have to leave today, Aaron comes with me."

Aaron felt a warm feeling which was swiftly replaced by anger. Who did Jake Brenner think he was, deciding what Aaron was going to do? It had been one punch. That was all. Aaron would be on the road within the hour. He was sure one of the other brothers would give him a ride into town.

Aaron pushed back the comforter and got to his feet. He gritted his teeth against another wave of nausea and headed into the bathroom. A brief shower and he'd feel like a new man.

"Aaron?"

"In the bathroom," he snapped at Jake's call.

Jake appeared in the doorway, his smile tentative. "You're awake."

Well, duh. Aaron forced a smile. "I'll have a shower and be on my way."

Jake frowned. "Where do you think you're going?"

"I need to find a job, remember? And you're going on the road."

Jake's expression changed. "You heard me talking to Alec."

"Yeah," Aaron said shortly. "I'll get out of your hair."

"You don't have to go anywhere," Jake said. "I've told Alec I'm not leaving you here."

"You've got a job to do." Aaron turned toward the shower.

"Aaron, I'm not leaving you behind." There was a touch of exasperation in Jake's voice.

"You're not leaving me," Aaron said. "I always intended to get going this morning."

"If we're going to be pedantic about it, it's actually this afternoon."

"What?"

Aaron turned so quickly he swayed. Jake was there in an instant to hold him.

"Hey."

Aaron just wanted to lean against Jake, but he pulled away. Shower. Then he'd be gone. He didn't want to be walking down the mountain road in the dark.

"You don't have to leave here before you're ready," Jake said.

Aaron gave Jake a bitter smile. "You don't have to feel guilty about getting me sacked. I'm used to being on the road."

Jake rolled his eyes. "I didn't bring you back here because I felt guilty. I brought you here because I didn't want you to die."

"As you can see, I'm alive."

Jake narrowed his eyes, and he pressed his lips together. Aaron took perverse satisfaction in annoying him, then he felt guilty. Then angry at himself for feeling guilty. Dammit, he was a mess.

"I don't allow my boys to be rude," Jake snapped.

Aaron raised an eyebrow. "It's a good thing I'm not your boy, then. Now if you don't mind, I need the shower. Otherwise, I'll be walking down the road in the dark."

He stared pointedly at the door. Jake turned on his heel and stalked out of the bathroom.

Aaron expelled a long breath and leaned against the frame of the shower stall. "You have to get out of here, Aaron, before you give away your heart."

He ignored the whisper in his mind. *Too late.*

At least the shower made him feel a lot better. He washed his hair and body, careful not to brush his various bumps, cuts, and abrasions, then leaned back, letting the hot water wash away the bubbles. He was tempted to stay there all day, but he was sure Jake would come find him soon enough. Aaron shut off the water and stepped out of the shower. He found a large, folded towel he was sure hadn't been there before. Jake must have left it without him knowing.

Aaron bit his lip. Had Jake watched him in the shower? Had he wished his hands were touching Aaron's skin, smoothing the bodywash and shampoo over his body? Aaron closed his eyes at the thought of his Daddy's hands on him.

He opened his eyes. Jake stood in the doorway, watching him, his expression hooded. Neither of them moved, then Aaron shivered, not sure whether it was cold or desire. Maybe both.

"I'm going to dry you," Jake said.

Aaron had a choice. He could say no, or he could submit just this once and let a Daddy take care of him.

Jake

Jake knew this was a mistake even as he picked up the towel and stepped into Aaron's space, seeing the boy shiver once more. The more involved Jake got with this boy the more he wanted him. Why did he have to meet Aaron now? But of course, Aaron had been there all the time. Jake had been too blind to notice.

The outside world would have to wait. Jake had a boy to take care of. He towel-dried Aaron's hair, not taking his eyes off him for a second. Aaron closed his eyes and seemed to melt into Jake's touch. Jake couldn't help wondering when the last time Aaron had received attention from anyone. He'd never seen the boy with another man.

Jake warred between wanting to haul Aaron into his arms and reminding himself he had no time to take care of a boy. Not even one as needy as Aaron. Their case had escalated from one evil nutjob to more than Alec and Jake had ever handled. They had rescued a hundred boys from the Mountain theme park, but now they were going up against a malevolent empire and Jake needed all his attention to get through the next month. He had no idea how long they'd be on the road. Maybe he could take Aaron's cell number and call him when they were back home. But what if Aaron was assaulted again? What if he found another Daddy? Jake gripped the towel tightly. He needed to take a deep breath. Aaron would move on, and Jake would rescue the boys.

Aaron shivered and Jake forced himself back to his task. Aaron's hair was partially dry, so Jake swept the towel down the length of Aaron's spine and around his taut butt. He imagined that ass blushing nicely after a sweet spanking.

He turned Aaron around so he could dry his torso. Jake dried his arms and patted the curls in his pits, his chest and abs. Aaron didn't have much body hair but enough to make Jake's mouth water. He liked body hair on a guy. He also like shaving it off and kissing the sensitized skin. As Jake paid him attention, Aaron's cock lengthened. Jake couldn't take his eyes off the thick shaft reaching out to him. A drop of pre-come emerged from the slit and trickled down the head. Jake had to press on his own arousal to stave off his climax. What Jake wanted was to sink to his knees and take it in his mouth, and make his boy come so hard he'd see stars. Then Jake would jack over him until he covered Aaron in pearly stripes, and he needed another shower.

Aaron's eyes were still closed, but he had his lip caught between his teeth. He was so turned on and unable to hide it. Jake reveled in Aaron being willing to show his vulnerability.

Jake took Aaron's dick in his hand, feeling the heavy weight of it and leaned forward. He swiped another drop of pre-come with his thumb. "I could stand here like this and make you come," he murmured.

Aaron opened his eyes, and the naked lust was there for Jake to see. "Yes. Do it!"

Jake didn't wait for him to change his mind. He'd never get another chance again. He jacked the shaft hard, and Aaron keened, coming up on his toes.

"Too much?" Jake asked.

"Not enough. More." Aaron's hands wrapped around Jake's biceps, holding him exactly where he was.

"I'm not going anywhere, my boy," Jake crooned. He was determined to drive Aaron wild, but they could take their time.

"Step one foot away from me and I'll have you," Aaron snarled.

"You're going to have me anyway, boy," Jake said calmly, "but it will be on *my* terms." He put his mouth against the shell of Aaron's ear. "It will always be on my terms...boy."

The shudder that ran through Aaron was very satisfying.

Aaron needed to remember who was in charge

41

of this relationship. Jake backed Aaron against the tiled wall. Aaron didn't take his gaze away from him.

"Hands against the wall," Jake ordered. "Don't move them until I tell you."

Aaron's chest heaved as he flattened his hands against the wall.

"Good boy," Jake praised. "Mouth or hand?"

"Wh—what?" Aaron took a moment to catch up.

"Mouth or hand? That's the only choice you've got."

"Mouth."

Before Aaron had even finished the word, Jake dropped to his knees and took that wonderful fat dick in his mouth, taking it to the back of his throat.

"Oh God," Aaron moaned as he tangled his hands in Jake's hair.

Jake pulled off and looked up. "Daddy."

Aaron stared down at him uncomprehending. "What?"

"Daddy, not God. That's all you have to think about. And hands against the wall. Now!"

Jake was sure Aaron said something uncomplimentary under his breath, but Aaron muttered, "Daddy," as he flattened his hands against the wall.

"Good boy," Jake said. He would deal with the attitude later. Now it was time for pleasure. He rested his hands on Aaron's hips and went back to driving him wild, taking Aaron's dick to the back of his throat again. He set up a punishing rhythm.

He didn't have time to draw it out. It didn't take long before he felt Aaron's thigh muscles tremble under his hands.

"So close," Aaron whimpered.

"Ask me if you can come, boy." His boy climaxing was his decision and his alone.

Aaron looked down at him, his eyes full of heat and passion. Jake felt the tension in his muscles. He so badly needed to come, wanted to ask, but desperate to fight Jake too. What would win out? Jake waited patiently.

"Please, Daddy."

That would do for now. Jake took Aaron to the back of his throat and sucked hard. Aaron yelled as he came in Jake's mouth, and Jake was sure it was only his hands holding Aaron up that kept him against the wall. Jake suckled him through his orgasm until Aaron whimpered and slumped over him.

"Too much," Aaron said.

Jake tugged his naked boy down to the floor. "What a good boy," he praised, pulling Aaron into his arms.

His boy leaned against him and shivered. Jake held him close to keep him warm and pressed a kiss to the top of his head. Aaron stayed where he was.

"What about you?" Aaron managed finally.

"I'm fine, boy. This was for you."

Jake meant what he said. He was aroused, his dick pressing hard against his jeans, but just being around Aaron had that effect on him. This time, he'd just wanted to make Aaron feel better. And to know what Jake could do for him.

"I should go," Aaron muttered against his chest. "I need to get on the road."

"I can't stop you," Jake said carefully, caressing Aaron's damp hair. "And if you insist, I'll drive you into town. Walking the mountain road is too dangerous, especially in the dark. But you're not going before you've eaten, and I'll find you somewhere to stay overnight. You don't want to be hitchhiking in the dark."

"I've done it before."

Jake was starting to realize Aaron's body told a whole language of its own. From the tension in Aaron's muscles, Jake realized the boy veered between asserting his independence and needing to be told what to do. He was going to have to handle Aaron very gently. Aaron wasn't a Kingdom boy and Jake had no idea what his life had been like up to now. If he'd spent his life on the road traveling from town to town, it didn't seem a stable one. He would have to investigate Aaron's background later.

He kissed Aaron's forehead. "I know, but you don't have to travel in the dark this time. Get dressed and we'll go find food. Then we'll talk."

Jake stood and tugged Aaron to his feet. "Do you like eggs?"

Aaron stumbled a moment until Jake steadied him. Then he blinked. "Uh...yeah."

"Great. See you downstairs."

Jake wanted to give his boy a chance to process so he gave him space. He pressed a kiss to Aaron's uninjured cheek and walked out of the bathroom.

Out of sight of Aaron, Jake took a deep breath. He really hoped Aaron didn't do something stupid, like trying to run away. But he would have to leave the decision to Aaron. Would his boy trust Jake to help him?

Chapter 4

Aaron

If he tiptoed down the stairs, he could get out of the cabin before anyone—Jake—noticed. He knew it was possible because he'd heard the brothers talking about it after one of their boys tried to run away. He wasn't sure why the kid tried to run, but he remembered the conversation.

Aaron dressed in the clothes he wore the previous day and went to pick up his pack. He furrowed his brow as he spotted something white under the dresser. He picked it up. It was a woman's sock with a pink frill around it. Why did Jake have a woman's sock in his bedroom? As far as he knew Jake was gay, not bi. Still, it wasn't his business. He put it on the dresser, then he tiptoed as quietly as he could down the stairs.

He could hear the low rumble of voices in the kitchen. Aaron couldn't help his smile. He could pick Jake's voice out from all the other brothers. By the time he'd almost reached the bottom, Aaron had convinced himself to make a bolt for it. Jake had enough on his hands without worrying about him. He wasn't keen on walking down the mountain road in the dark, but he could stay away from the edge, and how many vehicles would be going up and down the road at this time of day? He froze as the bottom step squeaked.

Immediately Jake appeared in the kitchen doorway. "Great. Come eat."

Before Aaron's brain had time to catch up, Jake took the pack out of his arms and left it by the door. Then Jake put an arm around Aaron's shoulders and steered him into the kitchen and to an empty seat at the table.

Gruff and Harry sat at the other end of the table, both working on laptops. They murmured hello and went back to whatever they were doing.

Jake poured him a large mug of coffee and a tall glass of apple juice. Aaron was somewhat bemused by someone pouring *him* drinks.

"How do you like your eggs?" Jake asked as he went back to the stovetop.

"Um, sunny side up," Aaron said.

What was he supposed to do now? He could hardly make a bolt for the kitchen door. Aaron had been so close to escaping. He'd been foiled by a squeaky floorboard.

Jake placed a plate of eggs in front of him and toast. Aaron's mouth watered at the smell of the homemade bread.

Then Jake sat next to him and took his hand. "Take a deep breath and eat. Don't make any decisions yet. I won't force you to stay. I just want you to be able to leave safely."

Aaron stared down at the eggs. "She did."

"Who?" Jake asked, clearly confused.

"My mom. She kept me locked up until my

eighteenth birthday."

The conversation died at the other end of the table. Aaron looked up to see the three men staring at him, but where Aaron had expected horror, they looked grim but resolute. Aaron guessed one strange mother didn't trump orphanages from hell.

Jake took Aaron's hand and squeezed it. "Eat your breakfast, boy, then we'll talk. Just remember we're not your mother and you get to make your own choices."

Aaron nodded and started eating. It didn't make him nauseated like the night before. "Good eggs," he mumbled.

"We have our own," Gruff said. "Lyle wanted chickens."

"And now I'm going to have to look after them while you go on the road," Harry grumbled.

"You never complain when you stuff your face full of eggs every morning," Gruff said and gave him a shove.

They bickered for a few minutes and went back to work.

"Just ignore them," Jake advised. "You can always ignore Harry, except when he's talking about horses. Then you listen to him."

"I've never been on a horse," Aaron said. "I'd like to try one day."

Harry beamed at him. "You can keep him, Jake."

Jake and Gruff both groaned.

"Did I say the wrong thing?" Aaron asked.

"No." Jake gave him a wry smile. "Harry is

always thrilled to find someone who wants to ride. Lyle loves it. Vinny doesn't want to go near a horse, especially Damien's horse, Thunder."

"No one wants to go near Thunder," Gruff pointed out.

"He's a sweetheart," Harry protested.

"You need your eyes testing," Gruff muttered.

"And you?" Aaron asked Jake.

"I don't have time to ride now," Jake admitted. "If it wasn't for Harry, my old girl wouldn't get a ride."

"Jake's mare is just right for you to learn on," Harry said.

Aaron gave him a tense smile. He wasn't planning to stay, so it was a moot point. Still, it would have been fun to learn.

"More eggs?" Jake asked.

"No thanks," Aaron said, "but thanks for breakfast."

"You're welcome." Jake topped off his coffee and sat next to him. "How are you feeling today?"

Aaron smiled at him. "Better than yesterday."

"Good." Jake hesitated before he spoke again. "We're not leaving today. Alec was just stressing about the road trip. We're gate-crashing Damien and Vinny's trip and they're not ready to go."

"When will you leave?" Aaron asked, trying to keep his tone bland.

"Two days. We'll go on Thursday."

Aaron knew what Jake was trying to say. He didn't have to leave tonight. But the longer he left it, the harder it would be to go.

Aaron forced a smile. "I gotta go. You could

drop me at the motel on the highway."

Jake gave a nod. "I understand."

Aaron was acutely aware of the silence at the other end of the table. He leaned forward. "If I stay, I'm never going to want to leave you," he whispered. He owed Jake his honesty.

"You don't have to leave me, boy," Jake said, taking Aaron's hands.

Aaron eased his hands out of Jake's. "I do. I have to find a job and you have to save hundreds of boys."

"You're the only boy I want to save."

Aaron gave him a sad smile. "I guess it wasn't my time to have the fairy tale happy ever after like Lyle and Vinny."

"We could. If you were willing to take the step," Jake murmured.

"And then what? Stay here while you traveled around the country saving other boys? I'd have exchanged one cage for another, Daddy. And what if you found another boy? You'd come home with him. What would happen to me?" Jake opened his mouth, but Aaron put a finger over his lips. "No, don't make promises you can't keep."

Jake sighed and leaned back in his seat. Aaron let his hand fall.

"I'll drive you down now if you promise to stay the night in the motel. I mean it, boy. I'll check with Rik at the motel that you're still there."

"Okay." Aaron knew Rik. The guy would be liquored up by eight. He wouldn't be able to tell if Aaron was there or not.

"Do you want to go now?" Jake asked.

Aaron nodded. He stood and looked at Gruff and Harry. "Good to meet you."

Both men nodded, but their friendliness had cooled. He had the distinct impression they disapproved of him leaving Jake.

"Take care," Gruff said, but his smile didn't reach his eyes.

Whatever. The Brenners would forget about him as soon as he walked out of the door.

Aaron left the kitchen and went in search of his pack and boots. Jake sat on a bench, lacing up his own boots.

"It's cold out there," Jake warned.

Aaron put on his boots and then his jacket. He didn't remember taking either of them off and guessed Jake must have done it for him.

Jake waited until Aaron picked up his pack. "Ready?"

"Yeah."

Jake opened the door and Aaron followed him outside.

Cold was an understatement. Aaron took a breath, and the air took an icy path down to his lungs. "Jeez," he muttered.

Jake led him to his pickup and Aaron climbed in, pleased to get out of the cold. Maybe he should buy an old pickup of his own. He'd learned to drive once upon a time. How hard could it be to drive again?

Jake eased out onto the mountain road. Aaron stared out into the darkness, seeing the lights of the town far below. His relationship with Jake was like this. Even though they sat next to each other, they were miles apart.

"I'm sorry," he said, out of the blue.

"What are you sorry for?" Jake asked.

"I don't know. Everything, I guess. Not being who you want me to be."

"I don't want you to be anything except yourself."

Aaron snorted. "I'm not sure who I am."

"You've been on the road for a long time," Jake said gently. "It's not surprising you've lost yourself."

"You're not the arrogant asshole I thought you were," Aaron said.

"Thanks," Jake said dryly.

Aaron felt his cheeks heat. "I'm sorry, I didn't mean—"

"It's okay. I'll live. I know I didn't cover myself with glory where you're concerned."

"It was my fault too," Aaron admitted.

"We were both idiots. I was trying to ignore you because I thought you hated me."

"And I was angry because you never looked my way."

"So why are you running away from me?" Jake demanded.

Aaron looked out into the darkness. The lights were much closer now. "I spent my life caged in one small room."

"You said it was your mom?"

"She wasn't well. She thought people were going to kill me because of my voice, so she locked me up in my room for my safety."

"Your voice?"

"She called me her songbird." Aaron turned at Jake's chuckle. "What's funny?"

"Have you ever heard the Brenners sing?"

Aaron furrowed his brow. "Uh...no."

"We can all sing, but I'm the songbird of the family."

"I haven't sung since the day I left." Even the thought of singing made him feel sick.

"How did you get away?"

"I escaped when I was eighteen. She was older and stopped concentrating as much. One day she forgot to lock my door. The front door was open. I ran out the door and never looked back."

Jake

Jake sucked in a breath. Dammit. This boy eviscerated his heart. "Is that why you keep on the road? In case she finds you and takes you back?"

"I'm never going back in that room again, Jake. Never!" Aaron yelled, then took a deep breath as if he were trying to calm down. "What if she finds me?"

"How long have you been on the road?"

"Seven years."

Aaron was twenty-five. He'd spent his entire adult life on the road. Jake's heart ached for his boy.

"Where did you live?" Jake asked.

"I can't give you that information. I can't take the risk." Aaron sounded miserable but resolute, as if he wanted to hand that burden to Jake, but he couldn't trust him.

Jake wanted to press him, but he didn't want to push Aaron away just as they were about to part. "I understand," he assured him, and felt Aaron relax a fraction.

He drove through the town to the motel. It was adequate. That was the best Jake could say about it. He and his brothers had stayed there many times when they'd sunk too many beers to tackle the mountain road.

Jake stopped the pickup in front of the reception and turned to look at his boy. "Are you sure you want to do this?"

At the hesitation, Jake's heart pounded with hope, but then Aaron picked up his pack.

"It's time I got on the road again," Aaron said. "Thanks...for everything. Take care...Daddy. Good luck with your case."

Jake sighed and nodded, squeezing Aaron's shoulder. "Come on then."

"You don't have to come with me," Aaron said.

"And if I don't, you're going to walk out of here and find a ride out of town tonight."

Aaron huffed and slammed the door shut.

Jake grinned. The mistake his boy made was thinking his Daddy was stupid. Then the smile slid off his face. He wasn't Aaron's Daddy. No matter how much Jake wanted it, Aaron wasn't his boy. Short of going down on his knees and begging, Jake didn't see how he could get Aaron to come back with him. But he could make sure Aaron stayed for the night in a bed before he got on the road.

He walked with Aaron into the reception,

ignoring the boy muttering under his breath.

Rik looked up and took a while to focus on them. Jake sighed. The guy was already liquored up.

Jake swore he heard a crow from Aaron, but he didn't look at him. "Evening, Rik. Have you got a room for the night for my boy here?"

"Oh hey, Jake." Rik swayed as he focused on Aaron. "Hi, Aaron. I thought you'd already left town. What happened to your face?"

"Someone took exception to my good looks and charm," Aaron quipped.

"Idiots," Rik slurred. "Good thing Jake found you. Take room 109. You know it, Jake."

"I do," Jake said cheerfully as he handed over his card.

"You know I can pay for myself," Aaron pointed out.

Jake patted his ass. "I know."

He led Aaron away from the desk, out of sight of Rik, and turned Aaron to face him. "I know what you're planning. I drive out of here and you get on your way."

Aaron's face tightened and he refused to meet Jake's gaze.

"Yeah, I thought so," Jake said. "Listen, you don't have to stay at the cabin, you don't even have to stay in town. Just do one thing for me and stay here overnight."

"Why do you care?" Aaron's voice cracked.

Jake ran his finger down Aaron's cheek, careful not to hurt him. "Because I do. Because under any other circumstances, I would be your Daddy and

55

you would be my boy. Because..." Jake took a deep breath. "I'm finding it really hard to walk away. But I will. I'll never cage you. But please, stay here overnight, so I know you're safe."

Aaron stared at him then, as if he were boring into Jake's soul. "You won't lock me up?"

Jake heard the echoes of a child locked in his room. "I'm not your mom. I'd never do that to you."

He waited a long time before Aaron nodded.

"I promise I'll stay here overnight." Aaron gave a long yawn and rubbed his jaw when it cracked. "I'm shattered. I need to sleep anyway."

"Call me when you're about to get on the road," Jake said. He handed the keycard to Aaron who looked at it for a long moment before he took it.

"You trust me enough not to walk me to the room?"

"You're an adult," Jake pointed out. "I can't force you to do anything."

He kissed Aaron on the forehead. "Good night, sweet boy."

Then he walked away.

It was the hardest thing he'd ever done. All his instincts screamed out to run back, take Aaron into his arms and never let him go. He wanted to do that so much. But he'd promised Aaron he would trust him and that's what he'd do.

He didn't even look back.

Jake waved at Rik who gave him a surprised wave in response, then headed to his truck. Once inside the safety of the cabin, Jake knocked his head against the steering wheel. Had he done the right thing? He had no idea. But he knew if Aaron was to ever trust him, he had to drive his pickup out of here.

He drove home in the darkness, forcing himself to focus on the road and not the beautiful, vulnerable boy he left behind.

The conversation died as Jake walked into the kitchen. All his brothers were there, large cups of hot chocolate in front of them. Vinny and Lyle sat on their Daddy's laps which made Jake's heart ache, but he forced a smile on his face.

"Hi, any dinner left?" he asked Lyle.

Lyle nodded and slipped off Gruff's lap. "Sit down, Jake."

"Where's Aaron?" Damien demanded.

"He's at the motel. He's gonna head out first thing tomorrow."

"Why did you leave him?" Alec asked.

Jake shrugged. "He wants to find another town and another job."

Harry scowled at him. "He's your boy. Why can't he stay here?"

Jake took a deep breath and looked around the table, warmed by the concern he saw on his brothers' faces. "Aaron wasn't my boy. Not yet. And I couldn't make him stay here. There are reasons. It's not my story to tell you. But he left for a good reason. Maybe if we weren't going on the road, it would be different, but he wasn't prepared to stay here while I was away. I asked him to sleep at the motel overnight and leave tomorrow."

Lyle slipped a plate of meatloaf in front of him together with a cup of hot chocolate. "You did the right thing, Jake." He squeezed Jake's shoulder and went back to Gruff, letting Gruff pull him onto his lap.

Jake sighed at the intimate gesture he desperately craved. "I hope you're right because right now I feel like a piece of crap."

"I'm sorry, Jakey," PJ said. "I'll pay your dollar."

Jake hadn't heard anyone call him that in years.

"Thanks." He dug into his dinner because if he looked up at his brothers, he'd do something stupid, like cry. He was sure they probably knew that, because they were kind enough to start a conversation about the road trip and he could focus on something other than the way his heart was breaking.

Chapter 5

Aaron

Aaron spent the night staring up at the ceiling, his mind focused on the Daddy he'd left on the mountain. Sleep was a distant memory. At six in the morning, he gave up and went in search of coffee. He wasn't surprised to find Rik snoring behind the counter.

"Morning, Rik," he said loudly. He could have gone behind the counter and gotten the coffee himself, but this was Rik's business.

Rik jumped and opened one sleepy, red-rimmed eye. "Huh?"

Aaron leaned on the counter. "Morning. Coffee?"

"Sure." Rik stood, yawned, and rolled his shoulders. "Just resting my eyes for a moment."

Aaron made a non-committal noise. It was no business of his what Rik did.

Rik poured the coffee into a large takeout cup. "Creamer? Sugar?"

"Creamer, thanks, Rik."

He took a long swallow, feeling the hot coffee burn a welcome path through him. Then he looked up to see Rik studying him. "What?" he asked, somewhat self-consciously.

"You look like crap," Rik said.

"Thanks." That was a bit much coming from the local drunk.

"Where's Jake?"

"He went home last night," Aaron said, unsurprised Rik didn't remember.

"Oh yeah. I forgot. Why didn't he stay with you?"

Aaron managed a bitter smile. "He got me fired. I gotta get on the road and find me a new job and somewhere to stay."

Rik looked confused. "Why didn't you stay at the cabin?"

Aaron stared at Rik, not sure how much the guy knew about the Brenner boys.

Rik rolled his eyes. Which Aaron guessed answered the question.

"You know about them?"

"They ain't subtle," Rik pointed out. He grinned as Aaron snorted. "I get a lot of custom from the Tin Bar."

"I guess you do," Aaron said. He tilted his head. "You don't mind?"

Rik shrugged. "If they pay, I don't care what my guests are into. The Brenner boys are good customers."

Aaron grimaced. "I realized that when I got fired."

Rik laughed at him. "I told Pablo he was an idiot to fire you, but you should have thought about it. No one wants to upset the Brenner boys. They're good customers."

"Yeah, I should. Jake just annoyed me with the fight." Aaron sighed. "I'd better get on the road. Hopefully this time I'll find a trucker who doesn't object to who I sleep with."

"You go easy, son. Here, let me top off your coffee."

Aaron smiled gratefully at him. "Thanks, Rik."

"You're welcome."

Aaron went back to his room as Rik returned to his chair. He wasn't surprised to see Rik asleep when he passed him a few minutes later. Aaron gave a wry smile and headed out of the motel.

Time for a new adventure.

Except no one wanted to stop for him today. He was cold to the bone and ready to give up when finally an old Chevy drove past and pulled up ahead of him. It was going in the wrong direction, but maybe it would return later in the day. It wasn't like Aaron had a fixed schedule. He jogged over to the Chevy and looked in.

"Hi...oh." His heart sank when he saw the bright red hair.

"Good to see you too, dipshit. Hop in."

"Uh no. Thanks, Harry."

The last thing he wanted was to go anywhere with one of Jake's brothers. Now he understood where Harry was heading.

"You're almost blue. At least get in the truck and warm up."

Harry wasn't wrong. His teeth chattered with the cold. Still, Aaron hesitated.

"Get in. Don't get in. I don't care. But shut the

damned door. It's freezing out there."

It was Harry's irritation that made up Aaron's mind. He slid in and closed his eyes, sighing in relief at the warmth being pumped out by the heater.

Harry didn't move away, waiting a few moments before he said anything. "That's better. You don't look the color of the snow."

"No one wanted to stop today," Aaron said.

"Maybe that should have told you something," Harry pointed out.

Aaron scowled at him. "Yeah, truckers are assholes."

Harry laughed. "Maybe they are. Or you are."

"And that. Thanks for warming me up, but I gotta go."

"Have you eaten today?"

Aaron thought about it for a moment. The last thing he'd eaten was Jake's eggs the day before. All he'd had was the coffee at Rik's. No wonder he felt hollow inside. "Not today."

"Let's go eat," Harry suggested.

"Then you'll let me go?"

Harry gave him an amused look. "I ain't locking you up, boy."

Aaron tried really hard not to flinch but from Harry's sudden wary look he hadn't succeeded. "I'm not your boy."

"You're not," Harry agreed. "You're Jake's boy. And he should be the one having this conversation with you."

"I'm no one's boy."

Not Harry's, not Jake's, not his mom's. Aaron

was his own person. He always had been no matter how much his mom had kept him in her prison.

Harry barked out a laugh. "You keep telling yourself that."

Aaron was about to tell Harry to fuck off and get out of the truck, when Harry drove away, not giving Aaron a chance.

"Where are we going?" Aaron asked suspiciously.

"The diner. I'm hungry." Aaron's stomach rumbled and Harry laughed. "I'm obviously not the only one."

"My belly wants to eat its way out of my body," Aaron confessed.

"We'll soon be there," Harry assured him.

It was less than five minutes to the diner, and the waitress greeted them both by name when they walked in. It was a small town. There weren't many places to eat, and Aaron had been there many times when he couldn't be bothered to cook.

They slid into a booth. The waitress came over immediately to fill their cups and take their order. Aaron didn't bother looking at the menu and neither did Harry. He wasn't surprised they both ordered the breakfast special.

Harry yawned as she walked away. "Sorry, it's been a long day. I was up half the night with one of the horses." At Aaron's concerned look, he said, "She'll be fine."

"I'm sorry," Aaron said sincerely. "How did you end up taking care of the horses?"

"We've always had horses and I've always loved them. None of my brothers showed any interest. I wanted to be a veterinarian. But there was no money for school, and we needed to manage the farm. So I picked it up myself."

Harry sounded remarkably free from bitterness, considering he couldn't realize his dreams. Still, he'd always known he was loved by his family. Aaron couldn't help his own bitterness seeping in. His mom's love had come with padlocks.

"You haven't called Jake, have you?" Aaron asked suspiciously.

The last thing he needed was Jake thinking Aaron needed someone to take care of him.

"When the hell would I have done that?" Harry pointed out. "Anyway, Jake and Alec are sorting out the RVs for the road trip."

"How many do you need?"

"Two," Harry said. "We're all big men. And there are eight...seven guys going."

"You're not."

"Someone needs to take care of the horses and I'd be useless trying to save the world." Harry sounded way too cheerful.

Aaron risked a quick glance at him, noting his expression didn't match his tone. "Are you miserable at the idea of your brothers being away from home or you not going with them?"

"You're very perceptive," Harry said. "The first. We've never been apart. Jake and Alec spend nights away when they're on cases, but we've never been apart for any length of time. I guess we're all too codependent. Maybe this will be good for us."

He didn't sound convinced though.

"I think it's nice that you care about each other enough to want to live together." Aaron said.

It was obviously the right thing to say because Harry beamed at him.

"Do you have any siblings?" Harry asked as the waitress brought their food. "Thanks, Sheila."

Aaron shook his head. "I was an only child."

"I wanted to be an only child when I was young," Harry admitted. "Seven brothers can get too much, even in a cabin our size."

"What did you do?"

"I went out to the stables and talked to the horses. Brad blew things up. PJ chopped down trees. We all had our own ways of coping. Still do."

"What did Jake do?" Aaron asked curiously.

"He and Alec watched cop shows."

"But they became PIs?"

"Our parents died. They didn't want to move away." The sadness in Harry's voice was plain to see. "I think the couples will be building their own houses soon. They need more privacy."

"But you're all Daddies," Aaron said.

Harry shrugged as he speared a sausage link. "I know, but you know what it's like. It's hard to go full Daddy and give your boy the time he needs when the house is full of other people."

"I never thought about it like that." Aaron had never lived with anyone other than his mom.

"Eat your food before it gets cold," Harry said cheerfully.

Aaron nodded and started eating. The Brenners were all the same. Loved to bark out the orders. The breakfast special was so good, and when they'd finished, Harry insisted on ordering extra toast because the bread was good too. Aaron knew he had to be careful of his money, but he could manage one meal a day. It wouldn't do him any good to pass out through lack of food.

Harry proved to be an entertaining companion, without the frisson that existed between Aaron and Jake. It wasn't until they were drinking more coffee that Aaron checked his phone.

"I've got to go," he said, with a reluctance he didn't want to admit. "It's gonna be dark soon."

Harry sat back in the booth. "It's up to you, Aaron."

The urge to beg Harry to take him to his Daddy was almost overwhelming, but he just nodded and pulled out his wallet.

"Put that away," Harry said, glowering at Aaron. "Jake would never forgive me if I made you pay."

Aaron could have insisted but he just nodded. He needed to save every cent until he found a new job. "Thanks, Harry. Take care."

He turned and bumped into someone. "Sorry, I—"

"Where do you think you're going, boy?"

Jake

The call from Harry was exactly what Jake needed to hear. He'd been miserable from the time he'd gotten up. It didn't help he'd had barely any sleep and felt like he was running on fumes.

They were driving the RVs home when Harry's message arrived. Jake had asked Alec to check his phone. Alec had sighed before he read out the message.

"Taking your boy for breakfast. Diner."

Aaron! Jake's body lit up.

"Aaron's still in town?" he queried.

"Unless you've got any other boy I don't know about."

"I'll drop you at the diner," Alec said. "I'll take the RV home. I'll tell Harry to keep him there."

"Tell him we'll be there in thirty minutes," Jake ordered.

"I'll say forty-five. You're not going to kill us by taking the RV off the road."

Alec sent the message and then let Damien and Vinny who were in the other RV know what they were doing.

Jake grunted. Alec had a point. Still, he breathed a sigh of relief when the diner came into view.

He pulled into the parking lot and stopped the RV. "I'll see you later."

Alec nodded. "Go get your boy."

Jake looked at his partner and his best friend. "Thanks, Alec."

Alec gave him a serious look. "Just keep your head in the game, Jakey. What we're doing is too important to fuck up."

"Dollar."

"Yeah, yeah. Get your boy before Harry puts a saddle on him and starts riding him."

Jake grinned. He would have been furious at

the idea of any other guy riding his boy, but where Harry was concerned, Alec meant it literally. Harry was much more comfortable with horses than humans.

He jogged over to the diner and pushed open the door to see Aaron getting to his feet. Just in time. He saw the relief on Harry's face as he caught sight of his brother walking his way.

Aaron turned and crashed into Jake. "Sorry, I—"

"Where do you think you're going, boy?" Jake asked, reaching out to steady Aaron who stared up at him open-mouthed.

"What are you doing here?" Then Aaron turned on Harry. "You lied to me."

Harry shrugged. "You asked me if I called him. I didn't."

"Potato, potahto."

"He messaged me," Jake said. "And a good thing he did. Why are you still here?"

"No one stopped for me," Aaron mumbled.

"He was freezing, and he hadn't eaten all day," Harry said.

"Narc," Aaron muttered.

Jake nodded. It was time to go all Daddy on this boy's ass. "Thanks, Harry. You did the right thing. My boy is grateful even if he doesn't know it yet."

Aaron had the grace to look ashamed. "Sorry."

"We're going back to the cabin. You're coming with me tonight. I'll drive you to wherever you want to go tomorrow, boy, but I'm not letting you out of my sight until I'm sure you're safe."

Aaron scowled at him, but Jake was sure it was

more for performance than because he was genuinely annoyed. If anything, he seemed relieved. Harry settled the bill and Jake insisted on leaving the tip for the waitress. Then he guided Aaron out of the diner and toward Harry's truck. As Aaron shivered, Jake wrapped his arm around Aaron's shoulders.

"You're very touchy-feely," Aaron muttered.

Jake didn't take his arm away. "Not used to holding hands or anything in public?"

"Last time I mentioned I liked guys someone punched me and threw me out of his truck."

"Fair point. But everyone in town knows we're gay and not many argue with us."

There were a few, Jake knew, but his family had lived here all their lives and most people were at least civil.

"Where are the RVs?" Aaron asked.

"Heading to the cabin."

"You take them up that road?" Aaron sounded incredulous.

"The road isn't that bad. You just have to be careful."

"I wouldn't want to drive them," Harry said.

"You don't want to drive anything except a horse," Jake pointed out.

"True, true." Harry opened the truck and Jake helped Aaron in. He wasn't sure when Aaron's brain was going to catch up to the fact Jake wasn't giving Aaron time to protest. At the moment Aaron seemed content to let Jake do the thinking.

Harry got on the road and Jake pulled Aaron into his arms.

"You look tired," Jake murmured.

"I didn't sleep last night," Aaron confessed.

"Or eat."

Aaron raised his head. "How did you know?"

"You just told me." Jake put Aaron's head down again. "You had one meal yesterday and one today. That's not good for you."

Aaron sighed. "I've looked after myself for the past seven years, you know?"

"I know." Jake struggled to find a way to show Aaron he didn't want to put him in a cage. "Just let me take care of you tonight, yeah?"

Aaron was quiet for a long while and Jake wondered if he'd dozed off. Then he murmured, "I liked your bed better than the motel."

Harry snorted. Jake glared at him across the top of Aaron's head.

"I'm not laughing at you," Harry said to Aaron. "Jake's real fussy about his bed."

Jake huffed, but Harry was right. He'd spent more on his bed than on his pickup. When he came back home after nights away, especially on difficult cases, he needed to relax in his bed.

"S'good," Aaron murmured.

"Go to sleep," Jake soothed, holding Aaron closer.

Harry put on a classic rock channel and turned it down low, then they took the mountain road back to the cabin.

It didn't take long before Jake knew Aaron was asleep, from the drool on his shoulder.

"You need to put him on a leash," Harry murmured as they turned off the road. "He needs his Daddy."

Not 'a' Daddy. But 'his' Daddy.

Jake stroked Aaron's hair. It felt gritty and his boy definitely needed a shower. "He'll run away from me if I try to cage him."

"You're overthinking this, little bro. You're not caging him. You're taking care of him. Aaron's got the option to leave any time."

"I'm not sure he'll see it that way."

"Then you make him see that. It's what a partnership is all about."

Jake looked at his brother. "Partnership? I'm not sure…we've only known each other for less than two days."

Harry brought the truck to a stop. "You guys have been dancing around each other for months. Don't think the rest of us haven't noticed. It's like Alec and Matt. One day they'll quit fussing and fuck each other."

Jake agreed with Alec and Matt. Those two needed a time-out in a playroom to work out their issues. But he and Aaron? He didn't even know Aaron had feelings for him until yesterday.

"You could have told me," he grumbled.

"Where would be the fun in that?" Harry smirked at him and got out of the van.

Jake looked down at his sleeping boy. "Hey there, we're home now."

Aaron raised his head and blinked at him sleepily. "Don't have a home."

This boy knew how to make his heart ache. "My home will always be your home too," Jake assured him.

Jake got out of the truck, then held out his arms to Aaron. He half expected Aaron to fuss but he didn't, just leaning on Jake as they walked into the cabin. Jake pushed Aaron down onto the bench and helped him with his jacket and boots.

Aaron sighed. "Jake, could I go sleep in your bed? My head aches like a bitch."

Jake smiled at him. It was the first thing Aaron had asked for, even if it did cost Jake a dollar. He pulled Aaron to his feet and wrapped his arm around his shoulders. "You can have Tylenol and a sleep. There'll be dinner for when you wake up."

"I feel like I want to sleep for a million years," Aaron admitted.

"I think I might get bored waiting for you to wake up."

"A hundred years then."

Jake kissed his temple. "Tomorrow morning at the latest."

"Okay." Aaron sighed. "Tomorrow morning."

In Jake's bedroom, Aaron took the Tylenol with the glass of water. Then he turned to Jake. "Will you undress me please?"

Even Jake heard the unspoken Daddy.

Slowly Jake tugged off Aaron's clothes, including his briefs. Then he urged Aaron into his bed and covered him with the comforter. "Go to sleep, my boy."

"You've got to stop calling me your boy." Aaron yawned and closed his eyes. "You're making it harder for me to leave."

"Why do you think I keep doing that?" Jake whispered in his ear.

Aaron didn't answer, but his smile was enough.

Jake pushed back a lock of hair. "You're not the only one finding it hard to leave, boy."

He left his bedroom and found Alec waiting for him outside, his arms folded. Jake sighed. His brother was obviously looking for a fight.

"Downstairs," Jake ordered. He wasn't taking the risk of Aaron waking up and overhearing them again.

Alec's glower deepened but he stomped downstairs, and Jake followed him. Alec went into their office rather than the kitchen. This was business, rather than family, as far as Alec was concerned.

Jake shut the door, sat on the edge of his desk, and waited for Alec to explode. It didn't take long.

Alec folded his arms across his chest. "What the hell's going on, Jake?"

"Aaron needed somewhere to stay for the night," Jake said as mildly as he could.

"You could have paid for another night in the motel. And why didn't he leave?"

"No one stopped for him."

"So he says."

Jake frowned at him. "What's your issue, Alec?"

"You need to be thinking with your big head, not your little head," Alec snapped. "What if Aaron's a spy for Kingdom Mountain?"

Chapter 6

Aaron

When Aaron awoke, he found a folded piece of paper on the nightstand. He unfolded it and looked at the messy handwriting.

"If I'm not here, come downstairs. Ignore any shouting. I'm gonna use my brothers for target practice."

Aaron blinked. He was tired but that really didn't make sense. He was hungry though, so he rolled out of bed and got dressed, hoping Jake made good on his promise of dinner.

As he approached the kitchen, he heard a noise which made him jump. It sounded as if someone was banging the table.

"You don't know, do you. You have no idea who he is or why he's here."

Aaron wasn't sure which brother had said that.

"Gruff had no idea who Lyle was, but he still brought him home," Jake said icily. "And Vinny. Damien brought Vinny into our house. And who the fuck is Matt?"

"You found Matt," Alec pointed out. "You met him first and brought him home."

Aaron knit his brows. Had Jake been Matt's

Daddy?

"You think my boy is a spy. That's ridiculous. I might point out he's been working at the bar for over a year, long before Gruff found Lyle."

Aaron rocked back on his heels. What the hell? Alec thought he was a spy! Oh hell, no. He stalked into the kitchen and fixed Alec with a glare that should have skewered him to his seat.

"You think I'm spying on you?" he asked incredulously.

"You know about Kingdom Mountain," Alec mumbled.

Jake sat back in his seat with a satisfied expression and folded his arms.

"Because you used to hold meetings in the Tin Bar. I told you that you think bartenders are deaf. And waitresses. And motel staff." Aaron threw his hands in the air. "I'm not a spy. I'm a bartender. That's it. Nothing else. You can check me out if you must."

Alec pressed his lips together. "I did."

"You did what?" Jake roared, springing to his feet.

"I had to," Alec said defensively.

Aaron's heart pounded hard, and blood rushed in his ears. "And what did you find?"

"Whoever you are, you're not Aaron Yates," Alec said flatly. "You're a bartender just as you said, but you only go back seven years. The real Aaron Yates died in 2001 aged four years old. So who are you?"

All eyes were on him. Aaron wanted to run away, but they'd catch him easily and send him back to the cage. Then arms were tight around him, and he didn't know whether they were home or hell, but he hung on to the comfort.

"It's okay, it's okay," Jake murmured in his ear. "I've got you, Aaron. I won't let you go."

"That's what I'm afraid of," Aaron said, but he stayed where he was, because as scary as it was to be in Jake's arms, it was scarier to be alone.

He stayed there for a long time, until he looked up to see everyone had gone except Alec, Gruff, and Damien.

"Are you ready to talk?" Jake asked gently.

"It's none of your business who I am," Aaron said. "You could have put me in danger just investigating me."

"You're right. It isn't," Jake agreed. "But you can see why my brothers are cautious."

"And you?" Aaron demanded.

Jake kissed his forehead. "I don't care who you are."

"And that's what worries me, Jake. You're not thinking straight." Alec snapped. "I'm not sorry for checking you out, Aaron. We've done it for all our boys. But you're the only one who's come up with a big red flag. You're obviously not Aaron Yates, so why have you got fake ID?"

Aaron held onto Jake as tightly as he could. "I ran away from home."

"Why?" Alec asked.

"My mom kept me locked up in my room my entire life." He saw the disbelief on everyone's faces except Jake and Gruff. "She'd tell me tales of how bad the world was, and I needed to be kept safe. She said they'd come for my voice. Yeah, I used to sing like an angel. She called me her songbird. I was a kid. I didn't know it was bullshit." He ran his hand over his hair. "I used to have long hair like fucking Rapunzel."

"Two dollars," Gruff said.

Jake sighed, pulled out two dollars, and stuck them in a jar on the dresser. He saw Aaron's confused expression. "Swear jar."

Aaron nodded. "I cut my hair the day I ran away."

"When you were eighteen," Jake said.

Aaron hesitated.

Alec narrowed his eyes. "How old were you, Aaron?"

"I was thirteen." He saw the shock in the expressions around the table. "I hit puberty early and looked older than I was, especially once I grew a beard. He rubbed his hand against the stubble. "I worked in places that didn't care how old I was. I could have been six and they just cared I could do the job." He didn't want to ever discuss some of the jobs he'd done to put a meal in his belly. One meal a day had been normal back then.

"So how old are you really now?" Jake asked.

"In Aaron years or Rapunzel years? I'm never giving you my real name."

"In Rapunzel years."

"I'm nineteen, almost twenty. I've been on the road for nearly seven years."

Then he was hauled into Jake's arms again, being rocked like a little child.

"Aaron." Alec huffed. "Let go of him, Jake. I

need an answer to this question."

Jake's arms eased a fraction.

"Aaron, why did you come to the Tin Bar?"

"I got fired from the last job for throwing the boss's son out of the bar. The truck I used to hitchhike out of town got me this far. I decided I liked it enough to stay."

"You've got to quit throwing people out," Jake whispered.

Aaron managed a giggle which was really more of a sob. "I'll remember that for next time."

"There isn't going to be a next time," Jake said firmly. "You're nineteen. Underage."

Aaron shook his head. "Not as far as my ID is concerned. I'm twenty-five. And you can't prove any different. There's nothing wrong with being a bartender." He looked up to see Alec, Damien, and Gruff staring at him. "What?"

"You should stay with us," Damien said.

"He thinks I'm a spy," Aaron said, stabbing a finger toward Alec.

"No, he doesn't," Gruff said. "He was just worrying about his little brother getting his heart broken. He can huff and puff about the case, but it's Jake he's more worried about."

"He told me to stop thinking with my little head," Jake pointed out.

"Oh dear God," Aaron muttered, feeling his cheeks heat. "Why don't you all mind your own business? Alec, can't you focus on your own love life?"

Alec looked puzzled. "What love life?"

Aaron blinked, then glanced up at Jake. "He

can't be that naïve?"

Jake's lips twitched. "He really is."

"What are you guys talking about?" Alec said.

Aaron was about to tell him in no uncertain terms when Lyle came into the kitchen and frowned at the empty table.

"Where's Aaron's dinner?"

Aaron's belly rumbled at the thought.

Lyle turned on Alec. "Don't tell me you've been interrogating him without at least letting him eat first?"

Aaron grinned at the chagrinned expressions on the brothers' faces as Lyle scolded them. He didn't know much about Lyle and Vinny as they were too young to visit the Tin Bar, but he'd gotten the impression Lyle was shy and Vinny feisty. But it was clear Lyle ruled the roost in the cabin.

"We weren't interrogating him," Damien protested.

"Yes, we were," Jake said. "We made him relive something he'd long since forgotten."

Aaron buried his face in Jake's chest. He didn't want to contradict his Daddy, but he'd never forget what his mom had done to him. He never wanted to go back to the Rapunzel years.

"Come sit down, Aaron," Lyle said. "You need to eat."

"He can sit on my lap," Jake said.

Aaron was on the point of telling him where he could stick that order, when it occurred to him, he'd like to sit on Jake's lap. It would make eating difficult though. Then Lyle brought over his plate.

Aaron blinked. The plate was covered in dinosaurs. They reminded him of a plate he'd had when he was younger.

"Uh..." Aaron said.

"Lyle," Gruff sounded amused. "This is one of your plates."

Lyle looked at it and his cheeks went crimson. "Oh, Aaron, I'm so sorry. I wasn't thinking. I'll swap it over."

He went to pick it up, but Aaron stopped him. "It's okay. Food is food. I'll eat it."

Lyle smiled at him gratefully and then the kitchen was empty except for him and Jake.

"Thanks for not causing a fuss," Jake murmured as Aaron started to eat.

"Is Lyle a little?"

"He is, but he and Gruff keep that side of him private."

"And Vinny?"

"He's not a little. He and Damien are exploring what Vinny needs."

"What about Alec and Matt?"

Jake chuckled. "I have no idea what's going on there. They both seem lost in a world of their own." He stroked Aaron's head. "I'm going to shower you and wash your hair before you go to bed."

Again, Aaron knew he should be protesting, but maybe this was what he'd wanted all along. He wanted Jake to take care of him. He looked down at the dinosaur plate. "I don't like dinosaurs," he admitted.

"I saw your face when you looked at the plate.

Bad memories?"

"Good memories," Aaron admitted. "Before I realized just how bad it could get."

Jake

There had been moments, alongside feeling envious that Gruff and Damien had found their boys, when he pitied them both for choosing boys who'd been so badly abused. That had been tempered with knowing his brothers were absolutely the right people to take care of boys like Lyle and Vinny. But now he'd met a boy with complex needs, and he wasn't sure he was the right person to take care of Aaron. What he did know was that he wanted to try because Aaron deserved the very best.

He watched Aaron scarf through his meatballs and pasta with some amusement. "You can slow down, my boy. No one's going to take the food from you." Aaron mumbled something. "What was that?

"She used to."

Jake's amusement faded away. "Your mom?"

"Yeah. I don't know why because she just threw the food in the trash. Anyway, I've always eaten fast since then."

Jake sighed and said nothing more. What could he say that would make it better? Here was a boy who'd been caged up, escaped, found his own life. He was so much stronger than Jake would ever be.

"Do you want more?" he asked. "Lyle always has leftovers. You'll never go hungry in this house.

It's a good thing we're always active."

Aaron's eyes lit up. "Yeah, that would be great. You're so lucky to have someone who likes cooking in the house. I live on takeout."

Jake eased Aaron into the seat and went in search of the leftovers. He found a plate in the fridge with a label on it.

"This is for Aaron. Hands off, PJ!"

He snorted. "I've found a plate with your name on it."

"Really?"

He showed Aaron the label.

Aaron burst out laughing. "Does he always do that?"

"He does when he tries to take care of others. I've got to warn you though, you may not be able to cook, but you will be expected to help, including peeling the potatoes. Just ask Vinny."

Aaron looked unimpressed. "I'm no cook, but I guess I can peel a potato."

Now it was Jake's turn to laugh. "You know how many people live here?" He watched Aaron process the numbers. "Exactly."

"You've heard of mashed potato you can buy, right?"

Jake grimaced. "It just doesn't taste the same. And Lyle would have conniptions at the thought of processed food."

"Do you peel the potatoes?" Aaron asked pointedly.

"He does now," Vinny said as he entered the kitchen, Rexy at his heels as ever. "Everyone takes their turn at all the chores. I'm the king of the vegetable peeler, and don't you forget it."

"Fair enough," Aaron agreed and seemed to bask in the warmth of Vinny's smile. He bent to give Rexy a tickle behind the ears and the dog closed his eyes with pleasure.

Vinny turned to Jake. "He likes my dog and he'll peel potatoes. You can keep him. He's not like that other guy."

"What other guy?" Aaron stiffened, his tone like ice.

Jake groaned. "Did you have to mention him?"

Vinny smirked at him. "Sorry."

Anyone else, Jake would have made a crack about telling his Daddy to beat his butt, but Damien had made it very clear no one could use that language around Vinny. Jake contented himself with a growl which made Vinny laugh as he left the kitchen with Rexy.

"You've got another boy?" Aaron demanded. "Why didn't you tell me this?"

Jake sighed. How did he explain Ryan? From the way Aaron was sending daggers his way, he wasn't going to get away with not giving an explanation.

"Baby, he's a boy from another club Alec and I sometimes go to. He's a friend who has particular needs and no Daddy of his own. Sometimes he and I met up for a session because we were both unattached. It wasn't anything more than meeting both our needs."

"But Vinny doesn't like him."

Jake chuckled, quickly suppressing it when Aaron's scowl grew deeper. "I don't usually bring boys home, but Ryan came here once. He and Vinny clashed. They're alike in too many ways. Also he laughed at the idea of peeling potatoes. It's a big issue with Vinny. I didn't bring Ryan back again. Now we're together, I won't meet Ryan again."

Aaron pursed his lips. "You said Ryan had needs?"

"Yeah."

"Then you should still see him. All boys deserve help."

Jake shook his head. "That's very generous of you. You have a big heart, Aaron." Jake placed a hand over Aaron's heart. "But I'm a one-boy Daddy. I couldn't have sessions with other boys when my heart is only given to one."

He held his breath because they hadn't had that conversation before. But the tension seemed to flow out of Aaron and Aaron breathed again.

"You're saying you're my Daddy and mine alone?"

"I am."

Whichever way their relationship went, Jake would devote all his time to this complex boy. He had to remember the boy was a lot younger than he pretended. Nineteen. Barely older than Lyle or Vinny. Just a baby really.

"What about when you go on the road?"

Jake took Aaron's hands and looked into his eyes. "You could come with me?"

"On the road trip?" Aaron seemed startled at the idea.

"Yes." Jake had thought about it for a long time.

And the idea of leaving him at the cabin without his Daddy to take care of him was just unacceptable. "I don't know what we're going to discover," he admitted. "And you may be safer back here. You may decide you want to stay in a town and get a job. We don't know the future."

"No happy ever after for us?" Aaron asked, somewhat bitterly.

Jake pressed a kiss to Aaron's palm. He wasn't sure how else to reassure his boy. He was offering him a life together without strings. Wasn't that what Aaron wanted. "Maybe. The future is what we make it together, Aaron. What would you like to do?"

Aaron let out an explosive breath. "I don't know. I know I'm being unfair on you."

"You're uncertain. I get that."

"Would you take me to bed?" Aaron asked.

"I can do that."

Jake stood and tugged Aaron to his feet. Before Aaron had the chance to squeak, he swept Aaron off his feet, and they left the kitchen.

"The plates," Aaron said.

"I'll do them later. You're more important."

Aaron sighed and pressed his head in the crook of Jake's neck. "No man's ever said that to me before."

Jake understood his mom had said things like that, but her words were chains around the cage, whereas Jake was trying to show Aaron he was free. "I'll keep saying it to you," he promised.

The bed was still unmade but Aaron didn't seem to care as Jake laid him down in the wreck of the covers and immediately straddled his thighs, bending his head to kiss Aaron tenderly. He knew Aaron's face was still sore from the thumping he'd taken. If he could, he'd kiss all the pain and bruising away.

"I will never lay a finger on you that you haven't agreed to," he promised.

"Thank you, Daddy," Aaron murmured, sounding almost amused. "But now could you fuck me, because my dick is about to drill through my pants."

Jake laughed at his blunt honesty. "I can do that." He sat up and felt the hardness beneath him press into the crack of his ass. He hummed and pressed down, feeling Aaron hiss. "You do seem to have a problem there, boy."

Aaron nodded. "I do and I need my Daddy to do something about it."

"What would you like me to do? Hand, cock, or mouth?"

"I need you to stick your thick cock in my hole and fuck me into the mattress."

"I do like a boy who knows what he wants."

Aaron tugged Jake down. "I always know what I want, and I've wanted you for a long time." Their lips almost brushed as he spoke.

"You know that I'd no idea that you felt that way, don't you?"

"I do. I thought you were a player. You always had a different boy draped over you."

"I just never had the boy I wanted." Jake owed him that honesty.

"And now?" Aaron sounded strangely nervous.
"I have the boy of my dreams underneath me."

Chapter 7

Aaron

Aaron wanted to beg Jake not to say things like that. Not to give him false hope for a future he was unlikely to have. Aaron had survived on the road by not letting anyone near him, physically or emotionally. He needed to be strong, not vulnerable, but Jake was unlike anyone he'd ever met. He overrode all Aaron's defenses and promised to treat him with respect. And it wasn't just Jake, it was his whole damned family. Even Alec who'd been hostile, had confessed he was worried about his brother's heart being broken. Who did that? The Brenners, obviously.

"Hey, where have you gone?" Jake murmured.

Aaron blinked and focused on his Daddy. "Huh?"

"You seem lost in deep thought."

"I was thinking that you have the best brothers in the world."

Jake barked out a laugh. "This isn't a one boy, seven brothers romance."

"Who has the energy for that?" Aaron shuddered at the thought. "I'm a one-Daddy boy."

"We fit just right," Jake purred, nuzzling against

Aaron's uninjured cheek.

Aaron wrapped his arms around Jake's neck. "Yeah, we do. Keep reminding me of that."

"I will. But first I'm gonna do what you asked me to do and nail you through the mattress."

Jake sat up, resting his ass against Aaron's engorged cock. He stripped off his hoody and T-shirt. Aaron's mouth watered at the sight of his broad chest covered with chestnut fur, almost hiding his copper nipples. His Daddy was huge. In a family of huge men, it was easy to forget just how big his Daddy was. He easily made two of Aaron. Then Jake slid off and wriggled out of his denims and briefs.

Oh yeah, Aaron almost purred. His Daddy was fully proportional. At some point he would definitely have his mouth around that thick, gorgeous cock.

Jake raised an eyebrow. "Am I the only one getting naked?"

"I was just admiring the view," Aaron said with a cheeky grin. "I haven't seen you naked before."

Jake almost preened. "You like what you see?"

Aaron sat up and placed a kiss at the tip of Jake's cock, then he buried his uninjured cheek against the fur on Jake's belly. "I like what I see, Daddy."

Jake ran his fingers through Aaron's hair. "I like what I see too, but now I want to see more of my boy."

One sneaked kiss to Jake's dick again, then Aaron wriggled out of his clothes, until he was naked against the pillows. Aaron's breath was taken away by the naked adoration on Jake's face. Aaron had never seen anyone gaze at him like he was precious.

"Kiss me," he begged.

"Your face—"

"Can deal with a kiss," Aaron assured him.

Jake straddled him again and bent down to kiss him, this time their hard cocks sliding against each other. Jake's kiss was soft at first, no more than a brush of lips, but Aaron needed more than that. He parted his lips and teased Jake's mouth with his tongue, inviting him in. Jake groaned, then Aaron had his Daddy flush against him, covering him with his warm, furry body and kissing him deeply, his tongue exploring Aaron's mouth.

Aaron lost track of time as they kissed. He would have been almost content with that until he felt Jake move and his dick slide behind Aaron's balls. Aaron gasped; the sound captured by Jake's mouth. Then Jake grasped Aaron's cock and jacked him slowly.

Aaron pulled back. "If you do that, this isn't gonna last long."

He would be embarrassed if he came before Jake's cock was inside him.

Jake's lips twitched. "Sorry."

That sounded sincere. Not.

But Jake took pity on him, and he reached over to the nightstand to pull open the drawer. Aaron was faced with a chest of thick fur and a copper nipple that begged to be licked and tugged. The wiggle and groan he received from Jake was very rewarding.

"You're driving me wild, boy."

Aaron smirked. "Sorry."

"I guess I deserved that."

"How can I make it up to you?" Aaron asked.

Jake seemed to think about it for a moment. "Get on your hands and knees."

He moved off Aaron, and Aaron did as he was asked, turning over so he was ass up, resting on his forearms.

Jake's warm hand ran down his spine to cup his ass. "You're so beautiful."

Aaron shivered as a cool finger circled his hole. "You could have warmed it up," he grumbled, to hide what he was really feeling.

"It'll all be warm soon, I promise," Jake said hoarsely.

Aaron rested his forehead on his fists and waited. Jake didn't keep him waiting long. A slick tip of one thick finger pressed in. Aaron moaned and pressed back, needing more, but Aaron held him still with one hand on his hip.

"We go at my pace," Jake said.

"Yes, Daddy," Aaron agreed, afraid Jake would stop.

One finger dipped in and out, then there was a slight burn as a second finger joined it. Jake pushed two fingers in and crooked them. Aaron yelled at the top of his lungs, shutting his mouth abruptly when he realized the whole household could probably hear them.

"Don't hold back your sounds, boy. No one cares here." He punctuated his words with another thrust in.

Aaron nodded and moaned in appreciation of what Jake was doing to him. Two fingers became three and he was a mess of pleasure, his cock drooling onto the sheet below, but he knew he couldn't last much longer. "Need your dick," he ground out.

His channel clenched and he moaned again as Jake withdrew his fingers and wiped them on the sheet. Then before the loss got too much, Jake pulled him to the edge of the bed and pressed his cockhead against Aaron's hole.

Jake filled him up like no man ever had. It was almost too much. Aaron gasped as Jake pushed in, breaching the muscle.

"Too much?" Jake stopped, his hands smoothing over his hips.

Aaron dragged in a shaky breath. "Just need a moment." Jake stayed still, smoothing his hands over Aaron's ass cheeks, until Aaron said, "I'm good."

"You're more than good, boy. You're perfect."

Aaron closed his eyes. Jake had unwittingly echoed his mom's words, which would always end on "and that's why I have to lock you up."

But Jake didn't say that, and he couldn't see Aaron's face. Aaron opened his eyes and looked over his shoulder to see his Daddy, to ground himself. Jake's face was strained, his eyes glassy, and Aaron saw he was hanging onto his control by a thread. Aaron realized he was the one who had the control here. It was almost overwhelming.

Aaron ground his hips back against Jake. "Love you."

Maybe it was too soon. He didn't care. At the moment all he cared about was reaching his climax with Jake buried inside him.

Jake growled and pulled back almost to the hilt. Aaron moaned and Jake pressed in again, his furry thighs against Aaron's. Then it was as if Jake let go of his control. Aaron found himself pushed further up the bed with each strong thrust, then Jake would pull him back and they'd start over again. Aaron wasn't sure how long this went on for until his climax took him over like a tidal surge. He was knocked off his feet, unable to focus on anything except the need to come in wracking spasms. Jake hung onto him and somewhere in the shocks that ran through Aaron, he realized Jake was coming noisily too, pushing into him again and again until he was slumped over Aaron's back.

It was hot and sweaty, and the room was filled with the sharp scent of their come, and Aaron collapsed into a heap on the bed. Jake tumbled with him, and the breath whooshed out of Aaron. He lay sprawled in the wet patch, with Jake breathing heavily in his ear. Aaron didn't even have the breath to tell Jake to get off him. He was going to be suffocated by his Daddy, because they had fucked each other's brains out. Aaron managed a smile into the pillow. Maybe that wasn't so bad after all.

Jake

Suffocating his boy wasn't the best way for

their first time to end, but it took Jake a moment to get the energy to roll off Aaron and collapse at his side.

"I think you killed me, boy," he moaned.

"At least you can breathe," Aaron gasped. He stayed where he was, sprawled out like a starfish.

Jake caressed lazy circles on Aaron's sweaty back. "You made me lose all feeling in my limbs."

"Likewise. Fuck, Jake."

"We've just done that. I'm shattered. You might have to wait a bit longer for round two."

Aaron snorted, but he didn't move, and they stayed where they were until Aaron sat up and picked at the drying come on his belly and chest.

Jake scratched at some of the white flakes. "I think you need a shower, boy."

"I think you do too." Aaron began to laugh. "We're a mess."

He rolled off the bed and looked down at Jake. "Coming?"

"Been there, done that," Jake muttered as he climbed off the bed and followed his boy into the bathroom. Where had his boy gotten this energy from? It occurred to him that the small gap in their ages had increased exponentially. No wonder Aaron's recovery time was so good. He was only a teenager.

Still, Jake was Aaron's Daddy, and it was his job to take care of Aaron. He washed him from head to foot in the shower, feeling Aaron's body react to his attention, but before Jake could do anything about it, Aaron stopped him with a hand to his chest.

"Daddy, may I wash you?" The tentative look showed he wasn't sure of Jake's answer.

Jake would give his boy anything he wanted if it was in his power. He handed over the bodywash. Aaron squeezed bodywash into his palm and smoothed it over Jake's back. Jake groaned as Aaron's wash turned into more of a massage, working out knots in his shoulder muscles.

"Where did you get so good at that?" Jake asked.

"A job I had at a masseur."

Jake hesitated. "Is this going to be a story you don't want me to hear about?"

"I liked it there," Aaron admitted. "But it wasn't the kind of place you want to be working in when you're a fourteen-year-old gay boy. I realized too soon that I was supposed to provide the happy endings. And I wasn't gonna do that, so I left and found another job."

Jake turned to face Aaron. "At some point you need to tell me what happened to you because the last thing I want to be faced with is your past coming to haunt you and me not knowing how to handle it."

Aaron refused to meet his gaze. "I'm not sure I'm ready for that."

"But I am," Jake said. "Nothing is as bad as what we've already faced."

"You sure about that?" Aaron muttered.

"Have you eaten a poisoned apple?"

Aaron furrowed his brow. "Uh...no."

"Have you been kidnapped by an evil CEO?"

Aaron's lips twitched. "Not that I know of."

Jake pushed the wet hair back from Aaron's face, exposing the purple and black bruise. "Have you been abused and beaten by the people who should have cared for you?"

"Does being locked in a room count?"

"Yes, baby, it counts. But we can deal with it. You, me, my brothers, the boys. All of us can love and support you. You're not alone, Aaron. You have us too."

He saw Aaron's face crumple and he tugged his boy into his arms. He soothed and cuddled Aaron as he sobbed out his grief until the water cooled. "Come on, we need to get out before it goes icy cold."

Once again, he dried Aaron, but the boy was clinging to him, and it didn't make it easy. Finally, he enfolded Aaron in the towel, picked him up and took him into the bedroom. The bed was a disaster zone and needed remaking, so he put Aaron in the large chair.

"Stay there, my boy. I'm going to make the bed."

"I should help you," Aaron protested.

Jake kissed his forehead. "I can do it. You just rest."

It didn't take him long to change the sheets, and then he picked Aaron up and settled him in his side of the bed. The boy had only slept in his bed twice and yet he had a side already.

"You take good care of me," Aaron murmured. "Better than my mom ever did."

"I'll always take care of you, my boy," Jake promised.

Aaron opened one eye. "Are you coming to bed?"

"I'm gonna get water, then I'll come to bed."

Aaron hummed and closed his eye. Jake was sure he was asleep before Jake was out of the room.

In the kitchen Jake found a council of war. Matt was there too, which meant this was business. Jake saw the grim expressions on his brothers' faces.

Alec looked up with relief when he walked in. "Good. I was just coming to find you."

"What's happened?" Jake said. It was nearly eleven at night. Whatever it was, it was serious.

"Quinn said we've got to move."

Jake wanted to protest. It wasn't the time. Aaron wasn't ready for this. But he and Alec had started this whole event, bringing in the other agencies. He couldn't walk out now, just because his heart was tied up with Aaron.

He sat down next to Alec. "We're ready to go. We've gotten the supplies. We just need to load the RVs."

"We did that this afternoon," Harry said, pointing at PJ. "You're ready to go except for fresh food."

"I can do that," Lyle said.

He looked exhausted as he leaned against Gruff. He was barely eighteen, and he spent most of his time cooking for the brothers or traveling around foster homes, checking on the boys from the Kingdom Mountain theme park. At some point, Jake thought Gruff needed to rein him in, but that was for his brother to handle.

"No, I'll do it," Vinny said. "You need to sleep. We can get moving at first light."

Alec turned to Jake. "Are you coming?"

Three days ago, it wouldn't have been a question. Jake would have been furious at even being asked. Now though he had a boy to think about. But this was too important. His heart had to wait.

"I'm coming."

"And Aaron?"

"I don't—"

"I'm coming too," Aaron said.

Jake looked up to see a sleepy-looking Aaron enveloped in Jake's navy toweling robe. "Aaron—"

"You have to go. I get that. But I'm coming with you. If it doesn't work, then you can drop me somewhere and I'll find another bar."

Jake held out his hand and Aaron came over, wriggling awkwardly onto his lap, trying not to expose himself to the rest of the table.

"He's just going to get in the way," Matt said.

Jake turned to stare at him, as did the rest of the table, and Matt blushed.

"No offense, Aaron, but you're not one of us."

"He's my boy," Jake snapped. "That's all you need to know. More to the point, you're not one of us."

Alec looked furious, as if he were about to launch himself at Jake, when the table rattled. They all turned to see Gruff bang the table with his fist again. His brothers were as shocked as Jake was.

"Enough!" Gruff glared at them all. "Matt, you don't get to say whose part of our family and who isn't. Not until you fucking...yeah, yeah, dollar...decide whether you're one of us or not. Aaron's been through enough shit—dollar—in his life to understand yours. And you guys don't seem to realize how hard it must be for Jake. He's been leading this case with Alec and now his heart wants to be with Aaron. His priorities have changed. He doesn't want to put his boy in danger. But he will do, for Lyle and Vinny, and all the other boys. And you," he stabbed a finger at Jake who was as open-mouthed as the rest of them. "You know Matt is one of us, even if he and Alec are too stupid to realize it themselves. And you and Alec have worked together since you finished high school. You are best buddies. Fix your differences now!"

Jake stared at him. "Wow, a two-dollar speech and you told us all off."

"Not me," Aaron murmured. "He didn't have a go at me."

"You didn't let me get that far," Gruff grumbled, his cheeks bright red. "I gotta speech for you too."

Aaron cocked his head. "Something along the lines of this case is too important to screw it up now?"

"Something like that," Gruff agreed.

"Way to go, little brother," PJ said, leaning over the table to ruffle his hair.

As Gruff opened his mouth, Lyle leaned in and hissed, "Don't make it three dollars."

Gruff closed his mouth with a sulky glare.

Matt bit his lip. "I'm sorry, Jake. I was out of order."

Jake pressed his lips together. "I'm not going to say it's all right, Matt, because it's not. But you're a part of this family whether you want to be or not. And I had no right to say any different."

"Can I say something?" Aaron asked, looking at Gruff who nodded.

Aaron looked around the table. "I know this is a difficult time for you guys. I know you all better than you think I do. Bartender, remember? I'll try not to get in your way, Alec. But I don't want to be left behind without Jake."

Alec gave him a nod. "I wouldn't expect you to. I was more worried you'd not be here when Jake returned."

Jake squeezed Alec's hand. They needed to talk, but his brother was still his best friend and always would be.

"I've got one problem with Aaron coming," Lyle said, and his scowl was fierce.

Jake stared at Lyle as Aaron tensed, clearly worried by Lyle's answer. Why would he mind?

"You didn't clear away the plates. That's not my job."

"See. I told you we should have done it before we fucked," Aaron said in a loud whisper.

Lyle snorted and he grinned. "Maybe you get a pass this once."

Chapter 8

Aaron

Aaron sat on the bed, his legs crossed, as he watched Jake move around the room, packing clothes. Aaron's pack was ready to go. Jake had ensured his clothes were laundered again while he was asleep.

"Where will we sleep?" he asked.

"We'll travel with Damien and Vinny, plus Rexy because Vinny won't leave him behind. Alec and Matt will go with Gruff and Lyle." Jake smirked at him. "Lyle and Matt were friends at the theme park."

"Weren't you taking one of the RVs?"

"We can all drive them. Well, not Vinny because Damien is teaching him to drive. And Lyle isn't confident enough yet. We've been loaned them for this case. They're huge. Can you drive?"

"Yeah, nothing like the RVs though. I learned with one of my jobs. I've got a license."

"As Aaron?"

Aaron knew Jake was having a hard time coming to terms with Aaron's true age. He knew it wasn't an age gap issue. Jake didn't have an issue with Damien and Vinny. And the age gap between him and Aaron was only eleven years.

"I could hardly put my name down as Rapunzel, could I? I was fifteen when I learned to drive. Plenty old enough."

"I guess not."

Aaron drew his knees to his chest and hugged them. "Do you have an issue with not knowing who I really am?"

Jake sat next to him and leaned against him as if he were the one seeking comfort. "No. Yes. No." He huffed. "Maybe."

"Getting mixed signals here, Brenner."

"Daddy. I'm your Daddy." There was an edge to Jake's voice and Aaron knew he'd stepped over the line.

"I'm sorry, Daddy," Aaron said contritely. "But I'm not sure what the problem is."

Jake turned to face Aaron. "I don't care you're nineteen. I ache for your life, as I do for Lyle's and Vinny's, but I don't care about your age."

Aaron took a breath. Okay, he'd just thought that, but it was nice to have it confirmed. "So what is the issue?"

"I can't keep you safe if I don't know the truth."

"You don't have to keep me safe," Aaron pointed out. "I keep me safe."

From the way Jake's jaw clenched, that wasn't the answer he wanted.

Aaron took Jake's hand. "I know the Brenner boys have a savior complex. Gruff saved Lyle from certain death. Damien kept Vinny out of the hands of the bad men. Alec desperately wants to save Matt from something. But me, I don't need saving."

"Except from icy deaths on cold roads," Jake pointed out.

Aaron frowned. He'd forgotten that. "So you've saved me. Can we move on?"

"But what if your mom turns up and I don't know who she is?"

"We're gonna be on the road. How will she find me?" Aaron pointed out.

He had that nightmare every time he went to sleep, but she'd never found him in seven years. Not even when he stayed somewhere for a long time like working at the Tin Bar.

"One day will you tell me?" Jake asked.

"When I'm ready," Aaron agreed. "You could call me Rapunzel if you don't like Aaron."

"Never gonna happen," Jake said flatly.

Aaron yawned loud enough to crack his jaw. "Can we sleep now?"

It was two in the morning. Jake had been too restless to sleep. Aaron wanted to keep him company, but now he was exhausted.

Jake pushed the hair back from Aaron's eyes. "I want to hold you in my arms while we sleep. Is that okay?"

"More than okay," Aaron agreed. "I need my Daddy."

His only real issue with going on the road was the lack of time to explore his boy side with Jake. He knew he was going to be with three other Daddy/boy couples, but would they get the chance to be in Daddy/boy mode? They were going on a mission to save the world, not explore their kink.

Aaron slid under the covers and rolled into his Daddy's arms. He rested his cheek on Jake's chest. "I can't wait for the bruising to go," he muttered. "I usually sleep on my other side."

"It'll be gone soon," Jake assured him. "The swelling is nearly gone already."

"Where are we sleeping in the RV?"

"Damien and Vinny will get the big bed. He's my big brother. I can hardly say no."

Aaron grunted. He'd gotten the hierarchy in the Brenner household.

"We can make a double bed in the living area," Jake said. "I'm too big for small beds."

"Good, because I'm not sleeping without you."

Jake kissed the top of his head. "You don't have to. I insist on sleeping with my dream boy."

Aaron's insides went all gooey at the idea of being anyone's dream boy. "What would you have done if I'd insisted on staying at the cabin?"

He felt the tension flood Jake's muscles and he pressed a kiss into Jake's chest. "This isn't a trick question, Daddy."

"I would have trusted my brothers to take care of you, but I'd probably be calling all the time," Jake confessed sheepishly. "Do you want to stay here?"

"I like it here," Aaron admitted. "I've never lived anywhere as nice as the cabin."

"Every time I think about moving away, I want to get back here," Jake said. "We're all too codependent on each other, but there's no one I'd trust to take care of the most important thing in my life more than my family."

Aaron took a moment to process that before he realized he was the most important thing in Jake's life. He raised his head, resting on his elbow as he looked at Jake. "You and me, we're still very new. I can't...give you my heart."

"You'll give it to me when you're ready," Jake assured him.

He wasn't sure he'd ever be ready, but he would take something on trust, and that was Jake's promise to take care of him.

Aaron let Jake switch off the lamp on the nightstand and rolled into his arms. They needed to sleep.

Watching the Brenner brothers say goodbye to each other was almost painful. Aaron stood back with the other boys. This was something just for the brothers.

"One of the reasons I love Damien is because he would give his life for his brothers," Vinny said.

"He fell apart thinking Gruff was dead," Lyle agreed. "They're all the same. It's why Alec fusses so much about Jake."

Aaron looked at the two boys. "Why are you telling me this?"

Vinny shrugged. "When I first met Damien, I thought he was a big, strong savior here to rescue me. I realized that he's all that and a sweet, gruff man with a heart of gold. He's never really been away from the mountain."

"None of them have except Jake and Alec,"

Matt said as he joined them. "You know more about the world than they do."

Aaron furrowed his brows, trying to get the point they were making. "You think that makes them weak?"

But the three boys shook their heads.

"It makes them strong, if maybe a little naïve at times," Lyle said. "We love them because they're like that. We didn't have childhoods in a loving family like they did."

"We didn't have childhoods," Vinny said.

"So their family is something we want," Lyle agreed. "Even Matt, if he won't admit it."

Matt spluttered but Aaron could see he agreed.

"Why are you telling me this?" Aaron asked.

"Because we know you had a childhood like ours, Aaron. You need the security of the Brenners as much as you need Jake."

Aaron wanted to deny it, but maybe they had a point. He looked over at the brothers. They were in a huddle, and he was sure Damien was at the center. Jake looked over at him and he definitely had tears rolling into his beard.

Aaron smiled at his Daddy. "So you mean, I take Jake, I take the family."

"And us," Lyle said.

"And Rexy," Vinny added.

"I should have kept my mouth shut in the truck," Aaron muttered.

"It was not keeping your mouth shut that got you fired in the first place," Matt pointed out.

Maybe Aaron had a pattern. Or he could just shut up.

"What happens when the other three brothers get boys? It's going to be very crowded in the cabin."

"Me and Daddy have a plan for that," Vinny said. "But first we've got to save the boys."

"Do you think you could be my friends?" Aaron asked in a small voice. "I've never had friends before."

"We can do that," Lyle agreed.

Aaron found himself the center of a huddle for the first time in his life. And yeah, there were tears.

Jake

Jake knew once big gruff Damien dissolved into tears it was inevitable the rest of his brothers would too. They all huddled together trying not to feel like they were tearing the family apart. Jake also kept an eye on Aaron who stood with the boys. They seemed to be discussing something. He wished he could have heard what it was, especially when they huddled together, but Aaron smiled at him, and Jake relaxed.

But finally they couldn't put off leaving any longer and climbed into the RVs.

"Fuck me," Aaron whistled.

"Dollar," Vinny said as he went past with Rexy.

Aaron sent Jake an appealing expression, but Vinny was right. Brenner rules applied even in here. Aaron was the only one who hadn't been inside the vehicles, so Jake understood his surprise. These were top of the range and huge.

Josh Cooper from Angel Enterprises had supplied them with a caveat that they were returned in one piece, or his husband would kill him.

"Traitor," Aaron muttered as he dug out a dollar from his wallet.

"Boy," Jake barked, and he saw Aaron's head snap up.

Oh yeah, his boy was going to learn that Jake wasn't that strict, but he didn't appreciate him being rude, especially where his family were concerned.

Aaron hung his head, seeming ashamed, and held out the dollar. "I'm sorry, Daddy."

Jake closed his hand around the bill. "Daddies are responsible for paying for their boys." Jake pulled out his own wallet and stuck a dollar in the RV swear jar. Yes, Lyle had supplied each RV with its own version.

He was sure that rule started because neither Lyle nor Vinny had money, but Jake would continue the practice unless Aaron's potty mouth got the better of his wallet. Jake wanted Aaron to save all his money in case something happened to him or them. The future was uncertain.

"What do you do with the money you save?" Aaron asked.

"We have a really good Thanksgiving," Jake said.

Aaron looked almost wistful. "I haven't had a Thanksgiving since I left home. I was always working."

Jake closed his arms around Aaron and tugged his boy against him. "Next time you'll celebrate with us."

"I'd like that," Aaron murmured.

"Take your seats," Alec barked. "We're on our way."

Jake pulled Aaron down onto one of the seats, who snuggled in next to him.

"Where are we going first?" he asked.

"We're heading to Florida. There's a Kingdom waterpark. The stories coming out of there haven't been good. Jake's jaw tightened as he thought of the information that had been fed back to him. "We thought the authorities would close down all the Kingdom parks, but not all have."

Aaron raised his head, his eyebrows knit. "And that's what we're going to do? Eight of us and one dog?"

Jake chuckled. "No. We're working with agencies across the country who are gonna take care of that. We're taking care of the boys. Making sure they go into good homes."

"You're going on a road trip to save some boys?"

Put it like that, it did sound crazy. But Jake had heard the unbelievable stories from Lyle of what was going on just up the mountain from their Christmas tree farm. He'd seen the disappeared who'd ended up dead in the Brenner woods. He'd seen photos of the tower where boys like Vinny and Lyle were abused day in, day out. Jake had lost his lunch the day he saw those photos, and Alec had gone into one of the barns and come out grim-faced and with his knuckles bleeding.

"They need us," Jake said simply.

Aaron looked into Jake's eyes. "Then I'm in. I could have been one of those boys."

Jake felt he was, in a way. But he loved his boy for understanding why this was so important to them. He caressed Aaron's cheek. "You don't have to do anything. I want you to understand that. Alec and I have to do this. Vinny, Matt, and Lyle lived this. You can understand why they're here. But my only worry is you are safe."

Aaron nuzzled into his hand. "I understand, Daddy, but I need something to do. Don't shut me out."

Jake hadn't intended to have this conversation so early, but at least he knew Aaron was on their side. He dragged Aaron onto his lap, and they snuggled together.

They'd sat in comfortable silence for a long time when Aaron said, "What did you mean, Ryan had particular needs? What kind of needs?"

"How much time did you spend watching the Daddies and boys?"

"I spent most of my time watching you," Aaron confessed.

Jake's heart melted. His sweet boy. "How much do you know about the ABDL community?"

"Not much," Aaron admitted. "I was behind the bar. I didn't see you interact beyond that."

"But you thought you might be a boy?"

"I thought I wanted to be your boy."

Jake held Aaron as close to him as he could. "Thank you. You don't know what that means to me."

"But you haven't told me about Ryan."

"I don't talk about my other boys. What we do is private," Jake said gently. He didn't want to upset Aaron, but Jake had prided himself on keeping his relationships private. He risked a glance at Aaron who seemed more thoughtful than upset.

"Was he a little?"

"A special little, yes."

Aaron nodded thoughtfully. "I found a sock under your dresser. A frilly sock."

Jake had no idea how Aaron could have found that. He'd packed up all his princess dresses, panties, and socks in a box to give back to Ryan. Maybe one sock had escaped. Aaron didn't seem angry though. "You're very observant."

Aaron hummed and leaned against him.

Jake wasn't sure what Aaron was thinking. "Is this something you've thought about?"

Aaron's hand clutched his. "You're not...disgusted by it?"

"No, baby, I'm not. I'm glad you felt able to tell me."

"I've never...tried."

"Not even in the bar?"

Aaron huffed in his ear. "You know what Pablo was like. I was there to serve drinks, not explore my kink. I don't think he knew or cared if I was gay or straight, as long as I could pour a beer."

"And you've never found a Daddy?"

"I did. Once. He wasn't like you. I didn't trust him." Aaron huffed. "I was only fifteen, although he thought I was older."

Jake had to repress a shudder at being caught

with an underage boy. Nineteen was hard enough for him to get his head around.

Aaron continued, unaware of Jake's thoughts. "He wasn't interested in helping me explore myself. He was more interested in what I could do for him. Once I realized that I grabbed my pack and left town. I've never found anyone who interests me since."

"Until you met me." Jake couldn't help the smugness in his tone.

Aaron rolled his eyes. "I was interested in you, but you didn't know I existed."

Jake kissed Aaron's temple. "I always knew, baby. I knew from the moment I walked into the bar and saw the new bartender."

"Could...could we get princess plates?"

Jake was thrilled Aaron was able to express his needs. "We can do that. You can pick the plates, or if you feel nervous, I can do it for you."

He wished Aaron had told him before they left. They had a stack of baby plates and cups in the dresser in the kitchen, including all the princesses.

"Will the others laugh at me?"

"None of my brothers will ever laugh at you or make fun of your needs, baby. We're all experienced Daddies."

He trusted his brothers implicitly. He wasn't going to tell Aaron, but Ryan hadn't been the only princess in their household. He knew Brad had been a Daddy to a little princess for a long time, before the man moved out of state. For a while Brad had contemplated following him but had decided to stay with his brothers instead.

"What about the boys?"

"They won't, but if they do, you tell me, yeah?"

"I will." Aaron seemed to melt against him. "You don't think any less of me?"

Jake held Aaron as tightly as he could. "Never. I'm not ashamed of you or me, or the world we live in. We're good men who like different things from other folk. I'm never going to be embarrassed about that."

"I don't think I could live as a girl all the time. I like being a guy."

"I understand, but we'll carve out girl time, Aaron."

"Anna."

Jake understood what Aaron was trying to say but he wanted to make sure. "When you want to be a girl?"

Aaron nodded.

"Anna is a pretty name." Jake wondered how close Anna was to Aaron's real name.

Aaron sighed and pressed his burning face into the crook of Jake's neck. Jake held him tight and crooned to him. Their conversation had taken a turn he hadn't expected, but it was good to be surprised by his boys. It kept him on his toes.

Chapter 9

Aaron

By now Aaron should have been in a new town somewhere, pouring beer, and getting Jake Brenner out of his head. Instead, he'd just been in the arms of his Daddy, confessing his secret desires, and now they were going on a potentially dangerous adventure. He had no idea how this was going to end. He wasn't in control, and this scared the hell out of him.

"Aaron?"

He looked up to see Lyle giving him a concerned smile. They'd stopped for the night and Lyle had coopted him to help cook dinner. They'd agreed to eat together. Aaron wasn't surprised to be handed the vegetable peeler. Vinny had vanished with Damien, supposedly to walk Rexy. He had no idea where Alec, Matt, Gruff, and Jake were, but nowhere near the vegetable peeler.

"Are you okay? You stopped mid-peel."

Aaron looked at the potato and then up at Lyle. "How can you be so calm?"

Lyle's smile was serene. "I have the love of my Daddy and I know whatever we'll find, it won't be as bad as I lived through."

Aaron didn't know whether Lyle was really that serene about the whole thing or lying through his teeth, but he could hardly call the kid a liar to his face.

Lyle sat down, picked up a knife, and started peeling a potato. "I know the whole thing seems strange to you, but Vinny and I, we'd be dead by now if it wasn't for the Brenners. You heard about being disappeared?" At Aaron's nod, Lyle continued. "I'd be dead if it wasn't for Gruff. Vinny was brutalized by the green coats. I want to spend the rest of my life in the cabin, taking care of my Daddy. But I can't leave other boys to suffer the same fate as we did. I have a responsibility I didn't ask for but it's important." They were silent for a moment, slicing skin from the potatoes. Then Lyle spoke again. "Why are you here?"

"I'm scared if I let Jake out of my sight, he won't come back to me." Aaron wasn't aware his hands were shaking until Lyle put a gentle hand over his. "Christ, I'm just like my mother." He looked up at Lyle in horror. "I want to cage Jake like my mom did to me."

Lyle gave a fierce shake of his head. "Let me tell you a secret. Jake didn't stop talking about you for weeks, months even. He talked about the bartender with the fierce eyes who didn't know he existed. He didn't know you were a boy. He'd have quit being a Daddy if it meant he could have you. You're not caging him any more than he's caging you. That's what being in a relationship is all about."

Aaron gave a wry smile. "I don't know much about relationships. My mom wanted to keep me locked up in my room for the rest of my life."

Lyle's expression was sympathetic but not pitying. "That's not what love is. You and Jake are right for each other."

"I thought the twinks draped over him were right for him too."

"They weren't you, baby." Jake bent down to kiss Aaron's lips. "Sorry for leaving you to do this alone. I had to go shopping. Are you nearly finished?"

Aaron looked at the potatoes in front of him. "No."

"I'll do them for you," Lyle said.

Aaron shook his head. "No, this is my job."

"I'll help," Jake said cheerfully, picking up another knife and a potato.

They were both faster than him. Aaron was an amateur. But they all worked through the pile while Aaron kept them entertained with stories of some of the dive bars he'd worked in.

"I'm lucky not to have lost you to a burly biker," Jake observed.

"Or a covert ops guy. You wouldn't believe one bar I worked in, in Wyoming. Howie was nice enough but Jake—another one—used to be covert ops. I moved on from there when they started asking too many questions about my ID."

"I couldn't tell it was a fake," Jake said.

"Nor me," Lyle agreed. "But then I've only just gotten ID of my own."

"These guys were scary," Aaron admitted. "I

liked the job, but I thought they might be working for my mom."

Jake looked at him speculatively. "You know Alec and I could find her. Your mom, I mean. We discovered who Vinny really was."

Aaron shook his head. "You start asking questions and she might find out where I am. I can't take that risk." The thought of her being anywhere near him made him want to hurl. At Jake's stubborn look, Aaron laid his hand over Jake's. "Please. I'm scared she'll drag me back."

Jake took a deep breath. "I promise you you'll be safe with me."

Aaron locked gazes with him and he'd almost forgotten Lyle sitting opposite him until Lyle coughed.

"I'm sorry, but I've got to finish these potatoes," Lyle said.

"We'd better finish," Jake grimaced. "It's a thing."

Aaron wasn't sure how peeling potatoes could be a thing, but he wasn't going to fight with his Daddy about it. He was coming to learn with the Brenners there were some lines you couldn't cross.

Jake pressed his thigh against Aaron's, and they finished the potatoes. Then Jake excused them both and took Aaron into their own RV, and led them into their bedroom. They'd decided to use a small bedroom to stow their gear, even if they slept in the living area because the bed was bigger.

They sat on the bed and Jake handed Aaron the bags.

"These are for you. You don't have to use them here, or you can do if you want to. It's up to you, but I'll respect whatever choice you make."

Aaron peeked in one of the bags and drew out a plastic plate and cup with princesses. "You bought this for me?"

"I did, baby. Just for you."

Then Aaron opened the other bag and stared up at him. "Daddy."

He drew out the soft, silky powder blue dress and white ankle socks with a blue frill. Jake had even bought him a pretty barrette.

"I know you've never explored this side of you, but I knew there was a store here."

Aaron had wondered why Jake had been so insistent on stopping here for the night when it might have made more sense to push on further.

"I'm not sure I can—here." The thought of dressing in something so fine in front of the others made his stomach churn.

"If you don't want to, we can wait until we get back," Jake said. "but I'd like you to try it on. Make sure it's the right size. You don't have to show me."

Aaron looked down at the dress. "Could...could you dress me, Daddy?"

Jake smiled at him. "I can do that." He leaned forward and locked the door. Then he tugged Aaron to his feet, tilted his chin and Aaron stared into his kind eyes. "I'm not embarrassed by your desire to be a little girl and I don't want you to be, hmmm?"

Aaron clutched at Jake's shirt. "You don't think

I'm wrong?"

"I think you're perfect, Anna," Jake assured him.

Oh, Daddy used his girl name. Aaron hadn't used it, even in his head. How had Aaron been so lucky to find this Daddy? Still, this was new and scary. But if he didn't like it, he could tell Jake he didn't want to do it again. Aaron took a deep breath and held out the dress.

"Please could you dress me, Daddy." He said it again to make sure Jake understood he was ready to take this step.

Jake stripped off Aaron's plaid shirt and white T-shirt, then he tugged his denims and briefs down his legs and pulled off his socks at the same time.

Aaron looked down at his legs. "The socks are going to look silly with my hairy legs."

"I can shave your legs, but only if you want," Jake said as he held out white panties. "I don't mind either way. Leave or not. As long as I'm the one who does the shaving."

Aaron nodded and stepped into the panties. It was something to consider later. The fact they had a later was something he could hug closer to him.

Jake tugged up the panties, then unzippered the dress. "Step into it and I'll zip it up."

Aaron did as he was told, and the silky skirt swished into place. He wished there was a mirror so he could see what he looked like.

"You don't have to wear just princess dresses," Jake said as he wrapped his arms around Aaron from behind. "I have a friend who makes all kinds of dresses for special boys. But I thought this was a good place to start."

"You bought something for me," Aaron whispered.

Jake nodded and pressed a kiss into Aaron's neck. "This is just the first of many, Anna. You are my special girl."

Jake

Jake wasn't surprised fate had steered him to Aaron. Lyle had needed a Daddy Charming. Damien had needed a boy to show him he wasn't an ugly duckling. Aaron needed someone who understood his deepest desires. Jake was a firm believer in soulmates. Look at Alec and Matt who obviously cared for each other, even if they were too stupid to admit it.

But when the silk had slid down Aaron's lean body and Aaron had obviously expected to be laughed at, then he'd known Aaron needed someone like him, who wouldn't laugh. He was gonna hug Vinny—with Damien's permission— just for mentioning Ryan. This had eased them into the conversation. The dress suited Aaron's dark coloring perfectly.

"We don't have much time now," Jake said, "but when we have more time, I know how to style your hair too."

"How did you learn all this?" Aaron asked, touching his hair self-consciously.

Jake bit his lip. "Brad taught me. I learned how to make all my boys feel good about themselves.

My brothers never made any secret of what they were like. So when I said I was a Daddy too, they taught me what they knew."

"You're very lucky," Aaron said, and for once there wasn't the usual hint of sarcasm he had when he discussed the Brenners.

"I am." Jake pressed his head against Aaron's belly. "And you're one of us now. You get the benefit of their experience."

"Most people get hand-me-down clothes," Aaron murmured, his fingers threading through Jake's hair. "Not kink experience."

"We're the Brenner brothers. We never do anything like everyone else."

Aaron snorted. He asked Jake to unzipper the dress which Jake was a little disappointed by, but he'd promised Aaron that he could take it at his own pace, and that's what they'd do. By the time Aaron was redressed—with some groping—and maybe a blowjob—or two—and the bags safely stowed in a closet, Vinny banged on the door, telling them dinner was ready. Jake straightened his clothing, then did the same for Aaron. He grinned at the dazed and happy look on his boy's face.

"We'd better get to the table before my brothers eat it all," Jake suggested.

Aaron nodded, but Jake could tell he was still come-drunk. He liked the look a quick blowjob gave his boy. He looked well-fucked, and Jake was happy for the whole world to know that was his doing.

As they went out of the bedroom, Jake caught

Aaron's sideway glance at the closet. He took Aaron's hand in his. "Maybe we'll have a meal in here by ourselves. We can use the plates then."

Aaron gave a quick smile. "Am I that obvious?"

"Just to me, boy."

Jake patted his boy's ass as they left their RV. It was a really great butt.

In the other RV, Vinny was talking ninety miles to the dozen about a dog they'd seen who'd try to scare Rexy. By the way Rexy was sacked out in front of the fire, on his back with four paws in the air, Jake guessed his owner was more bothered than the dog was.

"There you are," Lyle said, then he looked at the two of them. "Really?"

Gruff pulled Lyle against him. "What did I say about judging others?"

Lyle grimaced. "I should keep my mouth shut?"

Alec blinked. "Did you really say that?"

"Well, it wasn't as blunt as that, but yeah. We're three, maybe four, couples," Gruff said with a sly wink at Matt. "Who knows how long we're gonna be on the road? I'm not holding back on my sex life in case any of you are offended."

"Here, here," Damien agreed, and Jake was amused to see Vinny go crimson. It was obvious they'd gotten busy already.

Alec and Matt both rolled their eyes.

"We're not a couple," Matt said.

"Why not?" Aaron asked.

That question seemed to stump both Alec and Matt and they sat staring at each other for too long. Christ, it was painful. Jake thought they were idiots.

"We're meeting up with Quinn Ryder and Josh Cooper tomorrow," Alec said finally.

Jake looked at Aaron, seeing the tension in his face. Was it meeting new people that bothered him? "Quinn is a Daddy. His boy is Cade Connolly."

Aaron's mouth dropped open. "ConC?"

Jake chuckled. "I didn't know you were into art."

"Some," Aaron said. "Is Cooper a Daddy too?" He knit his brows in confusion as everyone burst out laughing. "What did I say?"

Jake took his hand. "Josh Cooper is more of a bossy bottom. He's not in our community. But he knows a lot of us who are."

"Doesn't stop him thinking he's in charge though," Alec grumbled.

"That's because he is in charge," Jake said. "It's easier to go along with what Josh says."

Alec grumbled under his breath, but Jake noticed he didn't disagree.

"Who should I listen to?" Aaron asked.

"Me," Jake said. "I'm the one that listens to Quinn and Josh."

He wasn't having his boy taking his orders from anyone else except him. He was relieved when Aaron nodded and leaned into him.

"I've gotten one piece of good news from Josh," Alec said. "Kingdom Theme Park in Georgia was closed by the authorities yesterday. The boys have all been taken into the foster system and the green coats are in custody. That just leaves five still operating."

Jake expelled a noisy breath. "That was one of the worst. How are the kids?"

Alec grimaced. "Josh says they were lucky to get there when they did. Some of the younger ones were half-starved."

"I should fly down there soon," Lyle said.

"One of Josh's teams is in there already. They'll liaise with you," Alec said.

He could see the conflict on Lyle's face. But the boy couldn't handle hundreds of boys around the country by himself.

To his surprise, Aaron leaned forward and patted Lyle's hand. "They've been helped. It sounds like the place we're going to needs you more."

Lyle bit his lip, then he nodded. "You're right. I just feel so responsible, you know? I'm the reason their world is being turned upside down."

"You can't carry that guilt, Lyle," Jake said as gently as he could. "You would have died if it hadn't been for Gruff. These kids would have died if it hadn't been for you. You're their savior, if a distant one."

Gruff shot him a grateful look. "I keep telling him that, but he still feels responsible."

Damien leaned forward and squeezed Lyle's hand. "If it hadn't been for you, I'd never have found the boy I love more than life itself."

Lyle stared at him, his eyes glistening, and Jake was sure Vinny sniffled too.

"This is all getting very Hallmark," Alec muttered.

"Four gay Daddies might just make it into a movie, but not with boys like us," Vinny pointed out with a smirk.

The conversation deteriorated into a possible plot which would definitely not be made by Hallmark. Even Matt joined in, and Jake noticed a moment when Matt leaned against Alec as they both laughed. Jake caught Gruff's eye. Gruff winked and Jake grinned at his oblivious brother.

Damien and Vinny disappeared into the main bedroom with Rexy, leaving Jake and Aaron to make up the bed in the living area. It was a queen-size bed and Jake was a king-size man as he kept pointing out, but when Aaron threatened to leave him alone and go sleep in the small bedroom by himself, he quit grumbling and tugged Aaron into his arms.

"You noticed Lyle's plate?" Aaron asked after they'd settled.

"Yeah, it was the dinosaur one."

"No one said anything."

Jake slipped a hand under Aaron's T-shirt and caressed a lazy line down his back. "I didn't expect them too."

"Maybe I could use my princess plate," Aaron said, but he sounded nervous.

"When you're ready, baby. And no one will say anything then."

Jake would make sure of it.

"You know, I thought about coming with you and asking you to drop me in a town anywhere. I'd find a new job, a new life. Safer because I'd still be Aaron and twenty-five. No one would know how old I really am or my past. Or who I want to be."

"What changed your mind," Jake asked. He'd known this was a possibility. Prepared himself for it.

"Because I knew if we were destined to be together, you'd drive back and find me. No matter how long it took."

"I would," Jake said.

"So I thought why do something that would make us both miserable? I'm yours, you're mine. And that's all that matters."

Jake rolled toward Aaron and entangled their arms and legs. "You know what, baby. That was a really sensible idea. I'd never have let you go."

"I have them occasionally," Aaron said dryly.

"Good boy."

Chapter 10

Aaron

Aaron side-eyed the two strangers at the table. On a scale of one to scary, the big, dark-haired guy managed an eleven. He made the four burly Daddies at the table look like huge teddy bears, which they pretty much were, Aaron had to admit. Quinn was dressed head to foot in black leather, which made him even more intimidating. It was clear Quinn Ryder was not to be messed with. The other man...Aaron had no idea what to make of Josh Cooper. No one could be intimidated by him. The man didn't shut up for one thing and he was always in motion. It was obvious Quinn was used to his companion, but everyone else, not so much.

"Every time I meet you guys, you have a new cutie," Josh cooed, holding onto Aaron's hand for a bit too long, and batting his eyelashes.

"Don't do that. It makes you look ridiculous," Quinn said.

"You're such a killjoy," Josh pouted.

"Aaron is Jake's boy. And you know what Cal will do if you act out."

From the way Josh's eyes lit up, he didn't seem to have a problem with that.

"Is Cal your boss or your boyfriend?" Aaron asked.

"Husband, boss, and my soulmate," Josh said.

Aaron eyed Josh skeptically. "And he lets you out on your own?"

Josh started laughing. "I like you, Aaron."

Aaron wasn't sure the feeling was reciprocated, just yet.

"Leave him alone, Josh," Jake said. "This boy is all mine."

Josh eyed them speculatively. "You need to meet Griff and Jem. I'll arrange it."

From Quinn's look of surprise and his sudden direct gaze at Aaron, Aaron had the feeling Josh Cooper was way more dangerous than he looked. He couldn't have guessed Aaron's secret, could he?

Jake didn't seem to react so maybe he was unaware what that little exchange meant. Maybe Aaron was reading too much into it.

Aaron was the only one not directly involved with the case, so he'd grabbed a coffee and curled up on the couch to watch the meeting. To his surprise, Rexy kept him company, but Vinny didn't seem put out, saying Rexy preferred to sleep on the couch.

Aaron kept the meeting supplied with coffee when one of them looked over. Still a fucking bartender. Aaron snorted at the thought.

As the meeting progressed, one thing became obvious. Josh was very much the guy in charge. He didn't force it, but even Quinn deferred to him. Aaron was kind of impressed, despite himself.

After a while, Vinny joined him on the couch, flopping down with a relieved sigh. Rexy abandoned Aaron to crawl onto Vinny's lap.

"You look tired," Aaron said, his voice low, seeing the dark smudges under Vinny's eyes.

Vinny grimaced. "Damien's not sleeping. He's freaked out by being away from home and what we're about to do."

Aaron nodded. He had a feeling of all the brothers, Damien would be the one to struggle. "Can I get you a coffee?"

Vinny hesitated. "Could you make it milk? In one of the plastic cups?" He said it defiantly as if he expected Aaron to laugh at him.

"Sure."

Aaron didn't care what people asked for as long as it was legal. He was a bartender. He gave people what they wanted. He poured the milk into a plastic Superman cup he found in the cabinet, topped off his own coffee, and returned to the couch.

Vinny murmured his thanks as Aaron handed him the cup. He took a long swallow, then wiped the milky mustache off his top lip. "It's been a long day. That dude never stops talking."

Aaron smirked, not needing to be told which dude Vinny meant. "Josh is scary smart."

"He is. But he keeps talking about everything that can go wrong and he's just freaking our Daddies out. I'm gonna spent tonight talking Damien off the ledge."

For a kid who had spent his whole life locked up in a theme park, Vinny was very perceptive about human nature.

"Maybe..." Aaron hesitated because it was the first time he'd ever suggested this. "We could have some Daddy and boy time. Either together or separately, before we go to bed."

Vinny gazed at him across the rim of the cup. "And how much does that scare you?"

"It freaks me out," Aaron admitted. "You guys are more relaxed about it than I am. Jake and I haven't had much time to play."

"Even though you worked in the Tin Bar?"

"It's different watching than taking part," Aaron admitted.

"But you thought you might be a boy?" Vinny queried. "Or you wanted to be Jake's boy?"

Aaron gave a wry smile and Vinny nodded. "I never wanted to be anything except Damien's boy."

"Did he tell you I told him to quit sulking and go home to his boy?"

Vinny smirked at him. "I should have guessed you were the one to cut him off."

"He was about to cause a fight. All the boys wanted to comfort him which was making the Daddies real unhappy. I told him to go home and sort it out with you."

"Thanks," Vinny said. "He did."

Aaron chewed on his bottom lip. "If I tell you something, will you promise not to tell Jake?"

Vinny nodded, his eyes alight with curiosity.

"This—" Aaron waved his hand at the men still talking at the table. "scares the hell out of me. I keep thinking it would have been easier to have been dropped off somewhere. This is above my pay grade."

"It's above all our pay grades," Vinny said. "You're a bartender. Lyle and me, we worked in the kitchen. Our Daddies sell Christmas trees. None of us dealt with men like the CEO."

"You always call him that," Aaron said.

Vinny shuddered. "I don't want to use his name."

Aaron understood that. He knew the power of a name. He hadn't used his real name since the day he walked out of his home. Once he'd earned the money to become Aaron Yates he'd never looked back.

"What I'm saying is I understand you're scared," Vinny continued. "We all are. But you don't know what it was like in there. We can't leave other boys to be disappeared or forced to become sex companions to the green coats."

Aaron prickled because he knew what it was to be caged, but he told himself to get over it. The least he could do was listen to Vinny. The more he knew, the better. Right?

After an hour of Vinny's story, Aaron felt sick to his stomach. No kid should ever have endured what Vinny and Lyle had been through. He wasn't sure about Matt, but Aaron knew Matt had been somewhere in there too.

"I get it," Aaron whispered as Vinny came to a halt. "No kid should be left behind."

Vinny looked gratefully at him. The boy was feisty and prickly, especially if he thought someone was muscling in on his Daddy, but he'd lived a life Aaron could never imagine. "We thought the Feds would handle it. They'd shut all the theme parks down and the kids would be rescued. But they've taken so long and there's a fightback from somewhere. Kids are disappearing or being trafficked."

"I'm sorry, Aaron," Lyle said as he sat next to Vinny. "I know you had your own problems. You shouldn't have to get caught up in ours."

Aaron gazed at them both. "Isn't that what family is for?"

Lyle nodded. "Yes, it is."

"And peeling potatoes," Vinny muttered.

Lyle turned to Vinny. "You've really got to get over that."

"Never."

Late into the night, Quinn and Josh left to find a motel, while the four couples made their weary way to bed. It was too late for Daddy and boy time. They were all exhausted and barely able to speak to each other. It was Aaron's turn to strip Jake and pour him into bed. Aaron turned off the lights and slipped under the covers.

Jake hauled Aaron into his arms. Aaron entwined their bodies together, willingly giving the comfort Jake seemed to seek.

"I never knew there was such evil in the world until Gruff brought Lyle home," Jake muttered.

"No one should have to find that out," Aaron soothed.

"Every time I speak to Quinn and Josh, I find

out more things I don't need to know. We thought we were dealing with one evil guy. We found out we were dealing with a nationwide cult. Me and Alec, we're country PI's, not spooks or bodyguards like Josh and Quinn."

He sounded so anguished, Aaron held him close, making incoherent soothing noises, and caressing his hair. "It's okay, Daddy. It's okay. You're not on your own."

"You're a joy," Jake muttered. "My little boy, my little Anna."

Aaron didn't know what to say. So he didn't say anything except hold his Daddy close. He knew if he had one role to play in this whole damned mess, it was to take care of his Daddy.

Suddenly a song came to him, one his mother had sung to him before things went bad. He started singing, stumbling a little, growing more confident as he remembered the words. Jake sighed and relaxed against him, as Aaron eased him into sleep.

Jake

Aaron was still asleep when Jake woke up the next morning. His boy was still used to working late into the night and sleeping late in the morning. He was asleep on his belly, one arm around a pillow.

Jake kissed Aaron on his shoulder blade, but Aaron grumbled and went back to sleep. Jake grinned and eased out of the bed trying not to disturb Aaron. The door to the main bedroom was open so he guessed Damien and Vinny had taken Rexy for a walk. It didn't bother him that he hadn't heard them go past. Jake had always been a deep sleeper.

He showered quickly and headed over to the other RV in search of breakfast and coffee. To his surprise he found Lyle in the kitchen, cleaning the cabinets.

"Morning," he said, helping himself to coffee from the pot and a pastry from the plate next to it.

"Morning," Lyle said shortly. It wasn't hard to see his brows knit together and his pinched mouth.

Jake chewed and swallowed before he replied. "What's wrong, little bro?"

Lyle wasn't his brother by blood, but he was part of the family.

"Nothing."

"Uh-huh," Jake drawled.

Lyle's head snapped up, then he sighed. "I'm sorry. It's not important."

"If you're upset, it is important," Jake said gently. "Is it Gruff? Have you had a fight?"

Lyle's tight expression eased, and he gave a genuine smile which made Jake relax. "Gruff is perfect."

"Then why are you out here scrubbing cabinets which are spotless?"

Lyle refused to meet his gaze. "I need time to be me."

Jake suddenly realized what he was trying to say. Lyle needed boy time, but more to the point, he needed time to be a little.

"Have you told Gruff this?" he asked gently.

Lyle huffed. "I didn't want to bother him. With this case, he's been trying to be so supportive. I didn't want to put extra pressure on him."

"I think you need to tell him, Lyle. He can't help you if you're hiding things from him."

"Tell me what?" Gruff asked, shuffling from the bedroom, his expression both sleepy and suspicious, his beard and hair sticking up at every angle.

Jake headed for the coffee pot and topped off his cup. "I'll leave you to talk to mountain man. Let me just get a coffee for my boy and I'll be out of your hair."

Lyle and Gruff stayed silent as Jake quickly poured another cup of coffee and topped it off with creamer, but as he reached the door, he heard footsteps. He turned to see Gruff enfolding Lyle in his arms. Jake smiled as he went down the stoop. His little brother could take care of his boy.

Aaron sat up, his eyes sleepy and hair in all directions, as he walked into the RV. "Is one of those for me?" he asked hopefully.

Jake handed Aaron the cup. Aaron took a long swallow and groaned in pleasure.

"I needed this. Thank you."

"You're welcome, baby." Jake gave Aaron a speculative look. "How would you feel about Daddy/boy time with Gruff and Lyle tonight? The Feds aren't making a move on the theme park until tomorrow morning. I think we could all do with something to think about other than what's going to happen."

"Is Lyle struggling?" Aaron asked.

Jake blinked at him. "How did you know that?"

"I didn't, but he's the little. It must be harder for him not to have time to relax with his Daddy."

"You're always so understanding," Jake marveled.

"There's a reason I was a bartender for so long," Aaron admitted. "I'm good at understanding human nature."

"I'm starting to realize that," Jake agreed. "Maybe that's something we need."

"I'm not a shrink," Aaron added hastily.

"You don't need to be. Just be there when we need to talk. Look how you helped Damien."

"Yeah, I cut him off and sent him home." Aaron grinned at Jake. "Vinny said thanks for that."

Jake grinned too, but then he sobered. "It's gonna be hard the next couple of months. People are going to need someone they can talk at."

Aaron grimaced. "Talk at. I get it."

"You're not directly involved. That's even better in a way."

"I'll help wherever I can," Aaron said. "Why don't we suggest a play date with Gruff and Lyle?"

"Do you want to go as Anna?" Aaron hesitated and Jake nodded. "You have a think about it."

"Thanks," Aaron said shakily. "What about the others?"

"I'll ask them to use the other RV. Baby steps, yeah?"

Jake could see the relief on Aaron's face and reminded himself never to take his boy for granted.

While Aaron showered, Jake sent messages to his three brothers. He got a yes back from everyone and a thank you from Lyle. He sent a separate message to Lyle and Gruff. He smiled at the immediate responses.

Aaron came out of the bathroom wearing just a towel wrapped around his waist, droplets of water caught in his chest hair. Jake's mouth watered just at the sight of him.

Aaron raised one eyebrow when he caught Jake staring at him. "Like the view?"

"Hell yes." Jake held out his hand. "Come here, baby."

Aaron walked over. "What do you want, Daddy?"

"You on your knees and your mouth around my cock."

"I like a man who knows what he wants," Aaron purred and fell to his knees.

Jake smiled up at the ceiling as a hot mouth engulfed his hardening dick. "You know just how to please me."

Aaron didn't answer. He was too busy sucking Jake's balls through his dick.

Jake held Anna's hand as Gruff and Lyle came in. Lyle wore a bright blue T-shirt and shorts with green smiling dinosaurs printed all over them. Lyle spotted Anna. Anna shrank against Jake.

"It's okay, my pretty girl," Jake crooned in her ear.

Lyle ran over and took her hands. "You look pretty. Daddy said I had to say that," he whispered with a grimace at Gruff.

Gruff rolled his eyes and Jake couldn't help chuckling.

"Come play with my dinosaurs. I've got girl dinosaurs too. You'll have to tell me the names though." He pulled a face. "I'm still learning."

Anna looked at Jake who nodded, then she left his side and followed Lyle to a rug Jake had put in front of the fire.

Jake caught Gruff's eye, and they moved away to let their littles play in peace.

"Thanks, Jake. Lyle really needs this," Gruff said. He lowered his voice. "He's really worried about tomorrow."

Jake handed Gruff a bottle of water and squeezed his shoulder. "Anna needed it too. You know how out of place Aaron has felt." He was still feeling his way through pronouns even though Aaron had assured him he didn't mind what Jake used when Aaron was Anna.

"You bought the dress the other day?" Gruff asked.

"I did."

"She looks pretty."

Jake looked over at Anna and smiled when she looked up. "Yes, she does."

He knew the line between Aaron and Anna was a fine one and he and Aaron still had a lot to explore. It didn't matter. Daddy Jake would be by Aaron's side all the way.

The playdate went well. Jake had made finger food that he and Gruff could feed to their littles.

Lyle twitched when he saw Jake cooking, but he managed to stay in little mode. Anna enjoyed being fed by her Daddy. Jake tucked that away for another time.

Lyle grumbled when Gruff finally said it was a little boy's bedtime. Jake had a feeling one little boy was looking forward to having his ass spanked by the fuss he made and the sudden excitement between Gruff and Lyle. Jake pushed them out the door and turned back to his own boy who was looking weary.

"Anna?" he said gently.

His boy shook his head. "I want to go to bed as Aaron."

Jake made up the bed in the living area. Then he undressed Aaron and put him to bed before he put the dress back in its bag for another day.

Aaron rolled into his arms as soon as Jake had gotten into bed.

"I want to tell you something," Aaron said.

Worry coiled in Jake's gut. Was Aaron going to walk away from him? Had this evening pushed him too far? "What do you want to tell me, baby boy?"

"My name was Andy," Aaron muttered against Jake's shoulder. "But I never want to be him again."

Jake held his boy as close as he could. "Thank you for telling me, but I'll never say the name out loud. That's dead to me. You're my Aaron and Anna."

Aaron nuzzled into Jake's chest. "Thank you for loving me."

Jake kissed the top of Aaron's head. "Always, my boy. Always."

"I know tomorrow's going to be a hard day for you all, but I'm here for you, Daddy."

"How could I have been so lucky to find you?" Jake marveled.

"Perhaps we should thank the truck driver."

Jake had other thoughts about what he could do to the truck driver who hurt his boy. "I don't think so."

"If it hadn't been for him..."

Jake rolled Aaron onto his back. He stared down at his gorgeous boy. "We'd have found each other. You and me...we're destined to have our happy ever after."

"Yes, we are," Aaron purred, and pulled Jake down for a kiss.

The End

Love from Sue Brown.

Next up is Jack's story. I already had the giant, but I couldn't work out how to fit the beans into the story. I decided to research one of the greatest loves of my life. Coffee. Ta-da! Problem solved.

Teaser from Jack's Giant.

PJ

PJ stared moodily into his hot chocolate, the ends of his untidy beard almost dipping into the hot drink. He barely noticed. PJ had made his mom's recipe, just as they always had, but it wasn't the same as Lyle's. Gruff's boy just made it better. But Gruff and Lyle were thousands of miles away, saving the world, and he was stuck here, on the farm, staring into a cup of hot chocolate.

The kitchen door opened and Harry, his older brother, stomped in, taking off his hat to reveal an untidy mop of copper hair. "It's cold out there. Thunder is sulking. Be careful if you go near him."

"Why would I be stupid enough to go near Thunder," PJ grumbled.

Thunder was his oldest brother's horse. They had the same temperament, growly and moody.

"What's your problem?" Harry snapped.

PJ didn't respond and Harry sighed, squeezing PJ's shoulder. "I know, I know. I miss them too, little brother."

"We should be with them," PJ said, leaning into his brother's comfort. He missed the bickering and the scuffles, the banter around the kitchen table. He missed Damien's grumpiness and Gruff going all Daddy Bear when he thought anyone was rude to his boy. Not that any of the brothers would dare to be rude to Lyle who took such good care of them.

"No, they should be here, with us." Harry gave one tight squeeze, then went to the stove to peer into the hot chocolate pan. He made a satisfied sound as he ladled two spoons into a cup with blue and white stripes.

Harry sat down at the table. PJ wanted to have his sulk in peace, but he knew Harry was struggling as much as he was. At least Harry had the horses to keep him company. PJ only had the trees. Not that he hadn't hugged one or two trees since his brothers went on the road.

"They'll be back soon, bro," Harry said, breaking into his thoughts.

PJ gave him a hangdog expression. "When? It's been a month and there's no sign of them coming back yet. Damien said Florida was awful. He's had to bring Vinny off the ledge."

"I know. He called me too."

PJ's lips twitched. "How many times has he called you today?"

"Two times before breakfast." Harry smirked at PJ. "And one more when he pretended he butt-dialed me."

"Me too."

"He's struggling worse than we are. Even Lyle's called once a day to see what we're eating."

PJ chuckled. "I swear that boy thinks we never cooked for ourselves before he arrived."

"I miss his cooking," Harry admitted.

"Me too. Even Mom's meatloaf wasn't as good as his. Not that I'd ever have told her if she were here," PJ added hastily. No one ever criticized their late mom without the other brothers falling on them like a ton of bricks.

Harry patted his hand. "I know what you mean. Mom would have loved Lyle. Especially as she didn't like cooking."

PJ furrowed his brow. "Mom loved cooking."

"Mom loved *us*," Harry contradicted. "Cooking for the family came with the territory."

"Wow, I never knew that."

"You were never in the kitchen long enough to find out."

It wasn't a criticism. PJ knew that. He'd always been the one by his dad's and Damien's side, running the farm. He'd always been closer to his dad than his mom. But PJ was feeling vulnerable today and the comment stung. He didn't want a fight with his brother though and he knew Harry meant well. "I miss Lyle's hot chocolate. It's always better than mine."

"Yours is fine but sometimes Lyle puts a pinch of chili in it," Harry said. "That's what gives it the bite."

"I've gotta spend more time in the kitchen," PJ muttered.

"You're doing just fine."

Now there was only Brad, Harry and him, PJ was the younger brother, and PJ had a feeling Harry needed to take care of him just to make himself feel better.

"Where's Brad?" PJ asked.

"Where do you think? He's in the barn."

PJ rolled his eyes. "There's nothing left to blow up."

"Brad can always find something to blow up," Harry pointed out. "But he's making repairs to the back wall of the barn. The last explosion went wrong."

All the brothers had their interests. Brad loved explosions.

Harry smirked across the table. "Did you hear he's been offered a book deal? A publisher read his poems and wants to publish them."

Explosions and poetry. It was a combination PJ couldn't get his head around. PJ was a guy with simple needs. A boy across his lap and a good IPA.

PJ stared at Harry. "You're joking."

Harry shook his head. "I'm not. Our brother is going to be a published poet."

"Grief," PJ muttered. He drained his cup and took it to the sink to rinse out. "I'm going into town to get supplies. Do you need anything?"

"I need toothpaste."

"Done." PJ didn't really need supplies. He just wanted to get away from the cabin. He felt as if the walls were closing in on him, even when he was outside.

Harry leaned back in his chair and looked up at his younger brother. "What about a trip to the Tin Bar tomorrow? It's been a month since the Brenner boys went in there to cause trouble."

PJ almost said no. Tomorrow was Tuesday. Daddies and boys night. But Jake wasn't there and he was the one who caused the most trouble. PJ shook his head to dislodge his gloomy thoughts. He needed to quit feeling sorry for himself and just enjoy a night out at the bar. "Yeah, why not," he agreed. "I could do with spanking a sweet boy's ass." There was a cute blond who always made a beeline for PJ. Sadly PJ didn't feel any spark for him, but he was happy to take care of the kid while he was there.

"Just make sure it's not that kid who tried to cause trouble for Jake. What was his name?"

"I don't think we ever found out," PJ said. "But I remember who he is. That kid deserves time out in the corner—permanently."

"He does," Harry agreed. "Still, if the brat hadn't caused trouble, Jake and Aaron would still be mooning at each other."

"Tomorrow we go to the Tin Bar and drag Brad with us."

Harry nodded. "Deal."

PJ headed to the hall to put on his jacket and boots. He would get the supplies, then go to the diner for a late lunch and a chance to catch up with his friend, Sheila.

"Brush your hair," Harry yelled from the kitchen as PJ opened the door.

PJ growled under his breath.

"Dollar."

"Later," PJ growled.

Like Harry had heard him. He was going to buy feed, not go on a date. But he stepped into the bathroom and quickly combed his hair, not that it made a lot of difference. PJ was way past due for Brad to give him a trim and tidy up his beard.

He stepped outside and raised his face to catch the late spring sunshine. He inhaled the sweet air and slowly exhaled. This was a good idea. He needed a break from the cabin.

PJ took a slow drive down the mountain road, windows down, blasting out country and western. His brothers mocked him unmercifully for his choices, but he loved it and didn't care who knew.

Buying the supplies took five minutes and he remembered Harry's toothpaste as he reached the truck. PJ was tempted to pretend he'd forgotten but he knew Harry would give him a hard time.

He returned to the store and purchased the toothpaste, along with a bright pink toothbrush because he was an ass, then got in the truck to head to the diner.

The parking lot was half-empty, but the diner seemed full. Sheila scurried between the tables as he walked in.

PJ waved at her. "Hey, gorgeous, you're looking real pretty today."

Sheila came over and he bent so she could kiss him on the cheek. "Afternoon, PJ. On your own today?"

"Yep."

"How're you doing?" She patted his back, her eyes sympathetic.

"Not good," he confessed. Sheila had known the family for years and knew how close the brothers were. She wouldn't laugh at a big guy like PJ missing his family. "I want to eat my weight in pancakes to forget."

She pointed him to a booth. "I'll be over in a moment with the coffee pot, hun."

PJ walked through the diner, waving at a few people he knew, rolling his eyes at the couple who blanked him. There were a few people who disapproved of his family. Seven gay boys was all wrong. He'd heard the whispered comments about not being brought up right. But his mom and dad had loved them all fiercely. PJ gave the couple the biggest smile he could. As far as he was concerned, folks who disapproved of them could take a one-way ticket on the next bus out of town.

He saw one face he didn't know, tucked into a

booth as if he were hiding. A young sandy-haired man, barely older than Lyle or Vinny. He looked tired, his shoulders slumped, as he drank a cup of coffee.

"Who's the kid?" PJ murmured when Sheila came over with the coffee pot.

"Came in on the bus," she said. "Never seen him before."

She topped off his coffee and vanished toward the kitchen, returning a few minutes later with a plate piled high with pancakes and an equally large stack of bacon. He saw the boy glance over, then quickly look away as PJ caught his eye. He was still just drinking coffee, no food in front of him.

PJ finished his lunch and glanced at his phone. It was time to make his way home. Sheila wasn't anywhere to be seen, so he headed over to the counter to settle the check. He'd pay for the kid to get a hot meal inside him too.

"Excuse me."

He turned, but as he did swung his arm out. To his horror, it connected with the blond boy. PJ was sure it was only a tap, but the kid collapsed, poleaxed, to the ground, and his head hit the ground with a sickening thud.

"What the heck, PJ?" Sheila yelled, rushing around the counter.

PJ knelt by the unconscious kid. "I hit him."

"I can see that, mountain man," she snapped. "The question is, why?"

If PJ knew that he wouldn't have done it. "I didn't do it deliberately. You know I'm a klutz and he was kinda in the way." He stroked the boy's hair away from his face, noting the creamy skin and long eyelashes fanning his cheeks. The boy had a light spray of freckles across his nose. He sure was a pretty one, but too pale. "Hey there, little one, time to wake up."

Also by Sue Brown

STANDALONE books
Summer's Dawn | Summer's Song | A Tale Told in
Darkness | A Cock in the Window | In-Decision |
The Backpack | The Clumsy Santa | Mr Plum |
Chance to Be King | Made for Aaron |
Final Admission | The Layered Mask |
The Next Call | The Night Porter | Light of Day |
The Sky Is Dead | Nothing Ever Happens | Stolen
Dreams | Waiting | Prey Time | Louis Hates
Valentines Day | Racing Raindrops |
The Fireman's Pole Falling for Ramos | Last Place
at the Chalet | Still Loving You

JT'S BAR series
His Shield | His Guardian | His Warrior | His
Valentine | His Protector | His Sentinel | His
Defender

BIKER DADDY BODYGUARDS
Hold Firm | Hold Close | Hold Safe | Hold Tight |
Biker Daddy Bodyguards Boxset

DARKER DADDY BODYGUARDS
Dark Heart | Dark Secret | Dark Haven | Dark

Angel

BEARYTALES IN THE WOOD
Snow Twink | Beau Bear | Boy Tangled | Jack's Giant | Boy Riding | Beauty & the Bear | Bear in Boots

ANGEL SECURITIES series
Morning My Angel | Goodnight My Angel | Hello My Angel | Angel Securities Boxset

LYON ROAD VETS series
Hairy Harry's Car Seat | Bob, the Destroyer of Leads | Hazel Takes Over | Stormin' Norman | Lyon Road Vets Boxset

DATING MR, RIGHT series
Speed Dating the Boss | Secretly Dating the Lionman | Slow Dating the Detective Dating Mr. Right Boxset

WITH A KICK series (with Clare London)
Hissed as a Newt | Bells and Balls

FRANKIE'S series
Frankie & Al | Ed & Marchant | Anthony & Leo |

Jordan & Rhys |

THE ISLE series
The Isle of... Where? | Isle of Wishes | Isle of
Waves | Isle of Waiting Island Doctor | Island
Counselor |Island Detective | Isle Series Boxset

SKANDIK & OWENS series
A Body in his Bed

MORNING REPORT series
Morning Report | Complete Faith | Go-to Guy |
Luke's Present | Letters From a Cowboy | Morning
Report Boxset

MULTI-AUTHOR
A Little Christmas! Danny
My Christmas Nemesis in Kind Hearts at
Christmas
Trickle of Blood in Gothika: Fang
A Boy Unleashed

About Sue Brown

Sue Brown is a Londoner with a dream to live on a small island. Coffee fuels her addiction for writing romance with hot guys loving each other, and her Adorkadog snores in harmony as she creates.

Come over and talk to Sue at:
Newsletter: http://bit.ly/SueBrownNews
Bookbub: https://www.bookbub.com/profile/sue-brown
Website: http://www.suebrownstories.com/
Facebook group:
https://www.facebook.com/SueBrownsStories/
Tiktok: https://www.tiktok.com/@suebrownstories
Email: sue@suebrownstories.com

Printed in Great Britain
by Amazon